Katherine's Web

Maureen Mitson was born in England and moved with her family to Adelaide as a teenager before her life turned around and she spent fifteen years living in various parts of the world. She has always loved writing and storytelling but only when she retired could she devote the time necessary to research her characters and their settings. She enjoys speaking of her life, writing experiences and how her books grow from an idea or an inspiration. She is active in writing groups and also leads a U3A poetry class.

Also by Maureen Mitson and published by Ginninderra Press

Paper Chase

Jumping the Cracks

Take Time… (Pocket Poets)

Insulae (Pocket Places)

Beatrice's Commonsensical Approach

Rupe (Pocket People)

Esther's Wars

Over the Rusty Gate

Maureen Mitson

Katherine's Web

Katherine's Web
ISBN 978 1 76041 581 5
Copyright © text Maureen Mitson 2018
Cover photo: Key to success © Sergey Nivens

First published 2018 by
Ginninderra Press
PO Box 3461 Port Adelaide 5015
www.ginninderrapress.com.au

The human heart has hidden treasures
in secret kept, in silence sealed;
the thoughts, the hopes, the dreams, the pleasures
whose charms were broken if revealed.

Charlotte Bronte, *Poems by Currer, Ellis and Acton Bell*,
The Floating Press

Katherine's Family

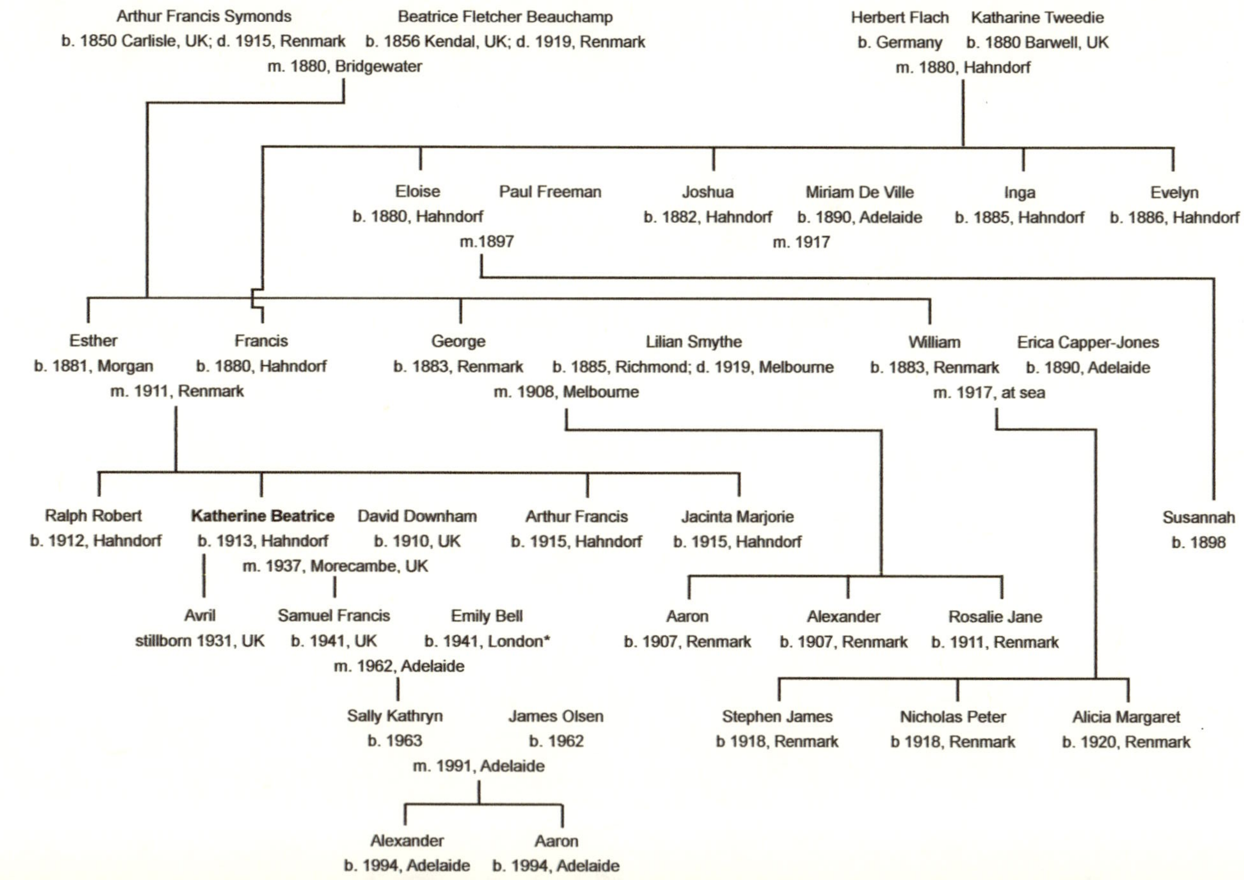

Prologue

Readers and writers are both sides of the same coin. Readers know the stories that appeal; writers hope to create the characters who engage. I've been a reader as long as I can remember and that led me to writing. When I create characters readers can identify with, are intrigued by, like or dislike strongly, I feel that I've realised my goal. One in particular felt like one of my family, she became so real to me and, it seemed, to my readers. I was asked often what happened to her after…? So I wrote a sequel and one of the characters involved in that story caught readers' imagination and I was inspired to further research; to dig deeper.

Deep is the word. This character, though a lovely person figuratively and literally, is hardly the typical protagonist of a full-length novel. Katherine lived an exemplary life, respectable and quite underwhelming. I began to switch loyalties, then a few cues came my way to make me realise she had developed the perfect cover – but for what? My writer's intrigue grew, yet on the surface this woman seemed the most unlikely protagonist.

I was only a child when I first befriended Katherine and she would've been in her fifties. She had long silvery-gold hair swept up at the back with a long comb that fascinated me. I asked what this long shiny thing with teeth was made of; she told me tortoiseshell. She elaborated, and for weeks afterwards I dreamed of a turtle encasing my own head, its claws – children's beasts are always well endowed with claws – scratching my eyes and ears! Then one day she showed me the difference between turtles and tortoises and I learned how fact should never give way to imaginative fiction.

Okay, I know that memory is itself a construction – particularly as it becomes distanced in time from actual events; interpreted by Mark Twain as 'never let the truth get in the way of a good story'. Hmm.

So, to the few cues I mention above: they were yielded by an old suitcase my mother found in my dad's cupboard after he died. She brought it round to my place, insisting I look into it – literally. Katherine was my dad's mother.

*

I gave her my frown and she responded in kind.

'Sally, please listen. Your dad had this thing tucked away among his other stuff and I thought it was just old socks and stuff to give to the shelter. Then I saw your Granny Kath's initials on it and found it full of old letters and…other things. You said you've nothing going on at the moment…'

'Mother! Thanks but no thanks. My writing isn't just a hobby, you know!'

'I know, darling, but you were named after her.'

No point refuting that argument; I am Sally Kathryn Olsen née Downham, wife of James, mother, ex-teacher now writer – and one 'with time on her hands'.

'Motherrrr! A ninety-eight-year-old lady with neatly tied silvery hair and a range of lavender wool cardigans…who liked nothing more than watching old TV soaps…and lived with you for at least half of her long life…whatever can she have in that old thing that's news to you? And the source of a good yarn for me?'

I let her switch on the coffee while I lifted the little case onto my gateleg table. She's obviously dashed a duster over the case but what she's left behind serves to highlight the name 'K.B. Flack'; aka my grandmother Katherine Beatrice Downham née Flack, now long departed.

Mum gave me that look again and handed me my coffee. 'Sally, your grandmother had a certain superior way of looking at things, as you know. Big on heredity and family bloodlines and prestige, all that. And as for the way she always spoke of her mother and grandmother as being "fine strong women of achievement" – okay, it stung. "Katherine daughter of Esther who was daughter of Beatrice…" and she thought me deficient, let's be honest.'

'Mum, that's ridiculous and you know it.'

She held up a cautionary finger. 'I wasn't good enough for her Samuel. Then I realised she had all those missing years and they, Sally, mean missing secrets! Big holes and big questions. Anyway, let's have a look in this case.'

She did make me a coffee. No way will I convince her that her own life story lacks nothing. She even commented at last Sunday's family dinner and, with no little envy, that a friend from her bridge group can trace her family back to a hanged bushranger who rode with Ned Kelly. To my mum, that's proof of a worthy existence, a rise above adversity, a qualification for Australian aristocracy.

So, while rabbiting on in my head all about this, not a little disgruntled by her attitude, I fiddle with the catches on this case. Must've taken effort to close. A dusty, perfumed papery smell hits my olfactory senses and I reach to dab and head off a sneeze. I nudge over the edge a little round tin can, about four centimetres across. Cursive labelling, 'Gibbs Dentifrice'. Tightly fastened lid, bit rusty round the edges. I held it up to Mum, who raised her eyebrows.

'Yuk. I remember that stuff, Sally. Pink powder...' She returns to my coffee machine.

I can check out the little tin can later and, oops! I catch the corner of a photograph with my cuff, one of those old-fashioned black and white pics with a curly edge.

Nothing wrong with my writer's reflexes, it didn't hit the floor. Who? Is it a doll? A very young infant? Compelling, for sure; a waxy face but beautifully modelled. Yep, it's a doll wrapped in a lacy shawl, and scrawled in ink on a corner, Avril.

Mum squints at the little pic. 'Avril? Don't know an Avril. You know, Sally, this might give a clue to all Gran's missing years.'

'What missing years?'

But with the usual waggle of fingers in farewell she's off. Hardly time to drain her coffee but just enough to burst my thought bubble. If I had one. Something constructive...

Sally

1

4 November 2017

I sit on my rocker with the cuppa and pull Mog onto my lap. He's always good company when I want to grumble. No prize breed, just a cat once too beautiful as a kitten to be left on the streets. I turn on my recorder – usual habit when I'm musing on a theme or trying out an angle. First, the date: Saturday 4 November 2017.

Trouble is, Mum's long had this envy – if that's the word – of my dad's lineage. There's no aristocracy, old-settler-worthy or whomsoever – not as far as I know. Granny Kath was simply proud of her roots, as they say. We heard little of family faults from her, of any lessening of standards, principles and ideals – but that was just her way. No spicy or gossipy stuff of the sort my mum longed to hear ever broke over her lips. Circumspect, was Mum's more polite description. I'm convinced she's dying to have Gran unmasked and the secrets of her missing years investigated.

What years were they? Before Gran moved to live on my parent's property in her little granny flat, she was a single mum and raised her Samuel, my dad, in a rented house in the western suburbs. I never heard my mum criticise her for raising Sam on her own. Why would she? He finished school, went to some accountancy or bookkeeping college and, it has to be said, he was a great dad to me. No degrees in management or anything, yet he built up a prosperous business. Mum helped run the office.

I do know Gran put money into the little granny flat they built for her after they married. I'm now in my fifties and dear old Gran lived there since before I was born, until she died when she was almost ninety-nine. 'A good innings,' proclaimed my cricket-loving dad. I still miss her.

'So, Mog, what secrets are waiting to be found? And what's mysterious about being a librarian? Especially one who always wore lavender-coloured cardies on cold days. She sometimes wagged her finger at my teenage stories but she was Granny Kath, trusted and friendly. I have to admit, as I grew older, had my boys and they grew up with their great-gran still in their life when some of their mates didn't even have grandparents, that was great. Real lap of the gods stuff. I still miss her and seeing her empty flat being now only another of my mum's projects hurts a little.

'She didn't like cats much. She inherited a stray but it was a scratchy beast and I don't think I ever saw her cuddle it, but she bought it chicken necks to gnaw on! Used to say to me that even cats deserve a cup of kindness now and again. Funny way of talking. We know she left to go to England in 1931: went for a year and stayed almost fifteen, as I understand it. Those are the only missing years but that's where she was a teacher. Had standards, principles – hated women wearing trousers but gave up barking at me when I explained about maintaining modesty among a class of primary kids. I know she upgraded her qualifications to include librarianship while her Samuel was little. And that's Gran – respectably uneventful, even dull. She was under Mum's eyes all the time they lived back here and yet she's still supposed to have secrets!'

Mog's response was to sneeze. I put him in the laundry out of the way and go back to the suitcase.

I riffle through some of the papers… Hmm. Definitely Granny Kath's handwriting; neat and tidy cursive. Ahah – some dates atop a page or two. Can determine a sequence… Well, that *is* something: 1929! Nearly ninety years ago. October and something else unintelligible. Hmm…quite a selection of notebook pages, single coloured notes. Worth a proper look.

I sat there, looking at the pile, feeling like an interloper. I can smell the deceptively gentle lavender soap, Granny's favourite, and it's been holding these papers together for – how long? Like she was maintaining a grip. Silly thought – these papers weren't hidden; she would have known Dad would look through them. And hers was a real sober-sides position; can't imagine her involved in any espionage, or even anything slightly shady! Gave up the volunteering when computers interfered and it wasn't her library any more. She was ancient by then, anyway. I used to visit her in her little house, we'd swap stories, I added my school newsy bits to hers. Then when I entered teacher training college in Wattle Park, she was so pleased she even shed a tear or two. As for when I actually started teaching, she announced herself chuffed to doll rags – one of her weird sayings.

I know she had once wanted to teach – 'then life got in the way'. She did do some sort of teaching, specialist stuff, but although she dropped hints and I waited for her to enlarge on them, nothing followed. She once visited a local primary school and spoke about Germany and took along some wonderful old carved wooden toys to show. I'd seen them but she kept them in a cupboard. In a drawer, she kept a folded German flag – one of the fancy ones with a crown on it. I found it while poking around one day and she was furious with me. Never saw it again. Gran didn't moan about fate or anything like that, was never overly critical of anyone or anything; she was just Granny and a friend to everyone. I could trust her with stuff I wouldn't tell my mum. She had a mischievous sense of humour – and her chuckle was so infectious.

That chuckle. Thinking of it brings back a memory; a special day. It was 10 August of the year before she died – that makes it 2010. Only a casual visit from me but turned out to be a lucky date; Gran brought out her Johnson's teapot with the big blue flowers on; no tea bags for us that day. She'd made some gingery biscuits, delicious. We sat on the old wicker chairs with the knobbly cushions in her sunroom and when I raised my eyebrows as Gran poured the tea into matching dainty cups with saucers, instead of our usual mugs, the little ceremony was explained.

'Your Grandad David would have been one hundred years old

today if he'd lived, Sally. All these years we could have shared. He never, ever knew my Australia, though I talked about it, often, and he so wanted to come over.'

I was momentarily lost for words but she held out the plate of biscuits. 'Have another one, dear girl. This is my mother's old recipe. My Oma Kate, Katherine Flach, showed us how to make them once, she called them *pfefferkuchen*. I used to bake them for your grandad and he'd take a batch whenever he went on a sortie.'

I was intrigued. 'A sortie, Granny?'

'You know he was in the Royal Air Force? That's the British one. He was a wireless operator in the war – the Second World War that was. Sortie was the word the pilots used. David learned on planes called Dominics – no, Dominies – specially used for training wireless operators. He wanted to fly on the Wellington bomber but instead he was made aircrew on a Whitley bomber, an Armstrong Whitworth Whitley. There were some Australian flyers on those aircraft too; they enlisted to go over to England. All brave lads.'

She almost grinned. 'You see, not all old ladies like me lose their memories! And for much of 1940 he seemed to be dropping leaflets over Germany, not bombs. They called it the Phoney War – I was so relieved, it all sounded less dangerous than I'd imagined. David was actually trained as a wireless operator and air gunner. But it was a very short period of training.'

She crunched one of her *pfefferkuchen* noisily, and only resumed talking after she swallowed the whole biscuit. I was fascinated. I'd heard little of this.

'David was based in the Midlands – somewhere around Birmingham, if I remember rightly. But we could meet when he came through to Kendal with others of his unit for parts or something. During his months at Driffield, I saw him only three times; very short visits made while their convoy passed through Kendal making for a base down south. That last time just after Christmas – Christmas '41, that was – he'd tried to get home for that and it was my birthday as well – they were to be sent out laying mines over the sea, after dark. It was the biggest hazard, he said. They had to fly so close to the water, apparently. That time he talked of living on borrowed time.

'His job was to send and receive wireless signals while they were flying and pass them to the pilot. But they usually flew at night and so he also helped his friend Peter, called an observer, I think, to spot enemy aircraft and somehow calculate navigational fixes. If they were attacked, though, he was expected to use their machine gun to fight off the enemy. Their weaponry was retaliatory only, defensive. That worried me dreadfully… Then they made him a sergeant, which thrilled him. He was so proud of what he was doing you see. They gave him a badge with a wing on it called a brevet to put on his tunic and I laughed because it had the letters WAG written on it. He was annoyed with me thinking it funny, but "wag" is a word my Australian papa used to describe someone who messed about a bit, you know, played the comic. What David was doing was not at all funny.

'You know, Sally, being the Jeremiah I am, I'd prepared myself for the worst possible news. Even before the war actually started, I feared the worst. Then our little boy had his first birthday and I took him for a studio photo to send to David. I still wish I knew that he received it – he'd changed bases. He was doing further wireless training somewhere, in fact helping with the training, and then moved elsewhere. I snapped later ones with my Box Brownie and he received some of them, I know that, but I didn't receive letters telling me he'd received all of them.

'Hmm. I remember how a bit later – was it 1941? Yes…it was all over the wireless that Rommel's Afrika Corps had attacked our forces in Tobruk. I was in a real tizz with worry about the baby coming and David being away so much but he came back for two days when he received the telegram about Samuel Francis hurrying into this world. I remember, he patted Sammy's head and said, "Fancy you arriving on the Ides of March, my son. I hope it's not an omen."'

My dad, wow. This was new to me. First time I'd heard her talk, really talk, of my dad when he was little.

She sat back in her squeaky chair. 'David was away a lot and I couldn't visit. Driffield was the home of Four Group, and I wasn't allowed there. He found it hard to find transport down to Kendal, too. I was…I was incredibly sad, that he couldn't know Sam, that Sam would grow older seeing so little of his father. Sam turned one then two and three and never really saw his dad for longer than a few days. We communicated mainly with letters, long ones, but he rarely answered my questions or responded to my comments. David was all about his work, you see. I so hoped he received that studio photo taken of me and Sammy when the boy was only a year old but he never said. I kept meaning to have another taken but I didn't. I had taken those photos with my Box Brownie, though, to send to his base.

'D'you know, Sally, although I missed David, I couldn't feel as upset for myself, as I knew was expected of me. I had prepared myself, you see. I felt a fraud, actually. In Sam, I saw David and knew he would always be with me in that way and, in a strange prophetic way, I sensed that was all I would have.'

She smiled ruefully. 'Not that I was reading the tea leaves! His task was not without danger, despite the newspapers laughing at the leaflet dropping. That was months earlier of course. No one took it seriously early on, I think they all thought Germany would capitulate or something. Mr Churchill of course cautioned that "a wave of perverse optimism" would only add to our peril. Then after Sam arrived, our life together became only a series of precious interludes in between weeks of loneliness. I was glad to have Sam for company at those times. And my mum, I so missed her. Even after…well, that's all passed. She did write now and again after I had baby Sam. More after my father died. He hadn't wanted me back but Mum…well, she was always asking me then why I wasn't shipping home. As if the seas were clear of danger! I knew only too well at that time how hazardous they were.

'Don't mistake me, Sally. I loved your grandfather in my own way but I was learning to accept what seemed to me the most probable outcome, that though he would always be a part of my life, he would not be significant in it. I was becoming a fatalist. It was a profound realisation and driven by the wartime situation. We'd been together not long at all before he joined up. Afterwards we saw even less of each other.'

Long talk. She refuelled, dipping another biscuit in her cup of tea and sucking it with gusto.

'He was such a good-looking man, my David. We met first in 1934, or was it '33? We announced our engagement quite promptly so he could – with a measure of propriety – take me to the Isle of Man to watch the famous TT motorcycle race. David loved the speed of racing! To my mind, he drove too fast on his own bike but he liked the fresh air round his ears, so he said. I think that was probably the first time in years that I'd written home and that was only because David insisted. Mum sent me a prompt reply asking me to be sure of my mind, asking who was this David? Each letter cost her a one shilling-and-sixpenny stamp then and the expense concerned me at times. I was so pleased when the aerogramme forms came into being later on – must have been towards the end of the war. Suppose I then felt less guilty. I should have been better, more prompt in replying, I suppose, knowing how things came about later on. I didn't answer every time, you see. There was a period when…well, that doesn't matter. It was an expense for me too and I was watching my pennies closely, as you would understand.

'When we married, we went on the train to Morecambe and he said the train was too slow! We hadn't been in a hurry to marry but I found out I was expecting and no way, no way, would I have anoth… an illegitimate child. Strange day, Sally. We married in a registry office there with my uncle and aunt as witnesses – rather hurried, really, but at least the deed was done and it was honourable. Then after all the rush, I had a miscarriage.'

'Oh, Granny!'

'Ancient history now, dear. David decided not to buy a motorbike, not even one with a sidecar. He said we'd save up for a car. I was not terribly interested in bikes and motors other than if they were a comfortable means of transport. David loved the bikes and knew all the professional riders' names of course. They were unimportant to me. He, your grandfather, loved speed, like I said. It seemed to fit with his later wish to fly planes. It was the planes that killed him in March 1942.'

Her voice broke, she coughed, sniffed and rubbed her eyes, then continued, 'David's plane was shot down while laying mines in the sea on what they called the U-boat lanes.'

I remember every detail of that afternoon in her conservatory, so rarely did she open up of her past life. At that point, she took a long sip of tea and gazed out at the garden, daydreaming…far away. I sat quietly sipping, and waiting. She spoke as if it was all only yesterday – not more than fifty years ago – talking of my dad as a baby, and how his dad, my grandfather, liked motorbikes. What's more, Gran knows a bit about bikes. Somehow can't see her sitting on one…doesn't fit the image. That's one thing I do know; the scar down the outside of her leg was from turning a corner on the motorbike. We'd been one day speaking of my son Alexander, how he wanted a motorbike to ride to uni, and she had been horrified! She told us David was taking a corner too fast and they were almost flat to the road, she said. Her knee was badly scraped and cut.

And that bit about her mother writing only after her father died… I was nonplussed, trying to work out what questions to ask, but I noticed she had that faraway look as she sipped the last of her tea

'You know, Sally, when they came to tell me about David, I was more worried about little Samuel. He had a fever. but he was well enough to yell and yell the whole time the policeman was at the door.'

'Policeman? Not an airman?'

She gave me a sad smile and handed me her empty cup and saucer. 'I'd moved back to Beast Banks, you see, and Kendal was handy enough to see David. I hadn't thought Samuel would be the last of the line, Sally. Shock, that was.'

Last of the line? Hey! What about Sam's grandsons? My sons? Surely… I turned round and she was already dozing in her chair. Dear Gran, she had talked a lot and I'd learned more about her life and feelings that day than ever before. She wasn't all routine and library books after all. Long letters, hmm. I made a quiet exit over to my parents' place.

Although years have gone by, yet that conversation with Gran was so rare and so fascinating I still remember it almost word for word.

2

So sitting here years later thinking of that phrase, memories being a construction, I wonder if I had heard Gran accurately. Did she almost say '*another* illegitimate child' that day? To my knowledge, my dad Samuel was her one and only, but she mentioned a miscarriage. When? Perhaps… I wonder could some of this suitcase stuff yield an answer or two?

I move to pick up that little snapshot of the doll. Mum knew of no Avril. So was Avril no doll, but a real baby? Its bonneted little face was perfect but it did look doll-like. I replace it on the suitcase. If a child, whose? Unlikely to have been Gran's. Mum could not have not known, had it happened. Yet I do feel her envy of Gran is at the bottom of all this missing years stuff; she hopes I'll discover some dark secret in Granny's papers, something that would render her less the matriarch of the proud and splendid line of heritage that even my dad liked to brag about. Strong women – well, who isn't? There were others before Gran, Dad liked to tell me, to instil in my teenage years an adult confidence perhaps, that I, also, demonstrated the fearless natures and resilience of those other women. Made me cross at times. I remember shouting once to him, 'I'm me! Myself! Not them!'

So, by analysing all this past chattering, I empathise, perhaps for the first time, with my mother's feelings. Did Gran have a darker side? What came before she and David met – or whom? And after he died? And why did her mother stop writing to her until after her father died? And her comments about her not responding to her mum's letters? Such an attitude seems a bad fit with the conscientious, so proper – if a little bit mischievous – grandmother I loved. And why didn't she write to her mother until she wanted to marry? Three years and no communication was not good. And is that right, that they were engaged for more than five years? I had thought everything was done in a hurry in that wartime. And her own mother, despite being within their religious enclave, surely there was contact of a sort?

And even so, Granny Kath said David was killed in 1942. Dad said it was about 1948 when Mum had bad news about her sister Jacinta and he was in grade two here in Adelaide. So where was Gran, and doing what, in those years?

I suddenly remember asking Dad why Gran didn't bring him home to Aussie straight after his dad was killed. Strange response: 'She had to follow her dreams, love. Wanted me to be old enough to meet everyone and to grow up knowing them as family.'

Fresh coffee to hand, cheese sandwich being relished, and Dad's voice in my head, I began chewing over the bread, cheese – and theory. How old had been old enough? Dad was born on 15 March 1941 and had to be here long enough to meet and fall in love with Mum; they married in May 1962 not long after his twenty-first birthday. Quite young. Familiar dates. I was born less than a year later, in March 1963. I think of them as being quite ordinary parents, content and accepting of whatever life threw at them, always – well, usually – supportive of me. Then Dad died of cancer in 2012. I remember him saying before he died that he was glad Granny Kath never knew of his illness.

She died the year before him. In 2011. When I was born, she was about forty-nine, yet she lived through most of the twentieth century and well into this one. She lived alone – independence was important to her – in her specially built little granny flat. That's how I remember her, doing what single older women do. Lovely silvery-gold hair, pulled up into what she called a chignon with long tortoiseshell hair combs. When I was smaller, I once asked them what they were made of and when she told me, I fantasised in more than one bad dream about little turtles crawling over her head and onto her face. I told her, so she brought me a book from the library all about tortoises – and about fantasies and facts. Even when I was a tiny tot, she would read to me.

Makes me think, surely such a lover of literacy would leave a journal. Maybe in this collection of stuff?

I drained my coffee. Predictably perhaps, as Gran aged and as I grew more worldly, I sensed in her another self wanting to escape from her trappings, to kick over the traces, to escape from an uneventful life. And perhaps she did find it uneventful, even boring. Yet there's no mystery in that. I remember her taking off on cruises with her friends up the river once or twice; she did a glamping trip with them at Yulara in the Red Centre – walked the nine kilometres around the base of the rock, Uluru, and came back full of tales about the mythology and mysteries of the experience. I'm sure I read her accounts in the library newsletter. That was before the baby Azaria was taken by the dingo; I remember when that story broke, Gran was too old to go off wandering any more but she insisted that dingoes did that kind of preying. Some of her friends who'd shared the glamping experience with her agreed. 'They're wild animals, Sally, and we can't change Nature.' I remember that comment because she then said how Nature was often cruel and it was a burden we had to bear.

Remembering made me sit up. She had endured a miscarriage; was that the Avril of the picture? No, that child was certainly full-term. Still…the question's there to be answered. I'll find that answer. It won't be too startling, I'm sure. Gran was a lover of TV soaps and romances and happy endings. She loved people, welcomed all visitors and she had a cat. Oops, better let Mog out of the laundry.

'Yes, Mog, Gran had a cat, one that found her and stayed. You wouldn't have liked him, though. I didn't. He used to spit at other animals and sometimes at people.'

Well, my snack is all gone, strong black coffee likewise. Too much of that lately; I'll be crawling up the walls at this rate. It's decision time. I'm a writer of stories: fiction with teeth, I like to say. So what is – was – Gran's story? Is there really a reason for my mum's envy, her feelings of inadequacy because of her own lack of history, of lineage? An outdated term, yet it seems to be so important to Mum and I think I'm beginning to know why.

Mum and Gran became close over the years; Gran declared herself the pseudo-Mum. Yet, after one rare occasion when Gran and Mum had words, and that was after I retired from school, Mum confided to me that Gran had accused her of being an unsuitable wife for her son. I thought that was a strange comment to make after so long together. I remember I made Mum a cup of tea that day because she was shedding a few tears and sniffing. I gave her a cuddle; I thought remarks like that would have been incredibly hurtful. Mum admitted, as she calmed down a bit, that she was so envious of Gran's background, her links with relatives and how she could claim a family tree – as Dad could – whereas she, Mum, had nothing like that to claim. I believe that one incident cemented Mum's notion she was deficient. I could understand but she, with my Dad's help, had risen above the brutality – as I later knew – of her early years.

When I did Mum's family history for her, with Dad's, I learned much of Dad's background too. I wrote the sequence, finalised the links and both were pleased. Dad said how my boys would like it perhaps – after he and Mum had gone. Ow! Dad's line through Gran goes back to the mid-1800s in northern England. Perhaps I could have traced further back but it wasn't needed. The name was Fletcher and they were farmers and quite well-off, or so I understood from Dad. That was Beatrice's family and her father paid for her wedding to a soldier who she later sailed to join in South Australia. She came out on one of the first steamships way back in 1879 and there was some incident that led to her marrying the ship's engineer, called Arthur Symonds. Beatrice was my Gran's grandmother.

They had a daughter, Esther, then twin sons William and George. Esther married Francis Flach when she was about thirty; he had a twin sister but I don't know much about her. Esther's children were Ralph, then Katherine, and then twins Arthur and Jacinta. Francis was of German heritage, a devout Lutheran and a master joiner. They lived in Hahndorf in the Adelaide Hills, built a successful business there and survived the unpleasant political and racial prejudices that were played out during World War One. That was an unpleasant period in our history and all because Australia was at war with Germany. Francis, ever prudent, changed the family name to Flack with a 'k', to avoid racial undertones; I noticed the spelling in this little suitcase.

What a sad situation. The uncle William who took the young Katherine and Rosalie with him to England was the twin of Rosalie's father, called George. The Symonds family farmed cumquats and grapes in the Renmark area and, as far as I know, their descendants still do. Sadly, Granny Kath is – or was – the only one of that family left alive till just before Dad died. So it's quite a family history but not an exceptional one for Australia. Apart from the indigenous Aussies, this country has been built by migrants. Mum was a migrant, one of the more unfortunate ones, and it seemed the basis of her despair was when Gran judged her inferior to Dad; called Mum too working-class, and accused her of being quick to marry Dad only to gain a decent name.

I knew Mum had come from England but that day she revealed – between sobs – how she had been born in South London and her home was flattened by a bomb called a doodle-bug during World War Two. She was found in a cot under a table in the London house and was the only one there who survived. She knows the doodlebug happened in June 1944, because it was written on her records in the home she was sent to. Those records showed her age as three; they gave her the name Emily because that's what it sounded like when they asked her and because she had a letter 'E' embroidered on her flannelette nightie. Emily she was called from then on. I pulled together the story for her and assured her it lacked nothing in the telling. Her father was a hero killed on naval service; her mother had been a nurse. The records I managed to find also showed that her mother and a brother were killed that night. She was saved by that solid kitchen table; she calls it by a fluke.

3

Too many names and all so far away in time and geography. It's now Sunday the 5th, and I'm sitting comfortably, cat curled on my lap, little recorder at the ready, in my air-conditioned Adelaide home. Morning broke when the boys tore off in their car to face their own day, a swimming carnival or something at one of the beaches. Quite sunny today, but not too hot; it's only November. I just hope Aaron doesn't burn, though – he always forgets the sun cream and with his hair colour…

So Katherine went to England, to stay for a year, in 1931 and didn't return to Australia until Dad was at school. His was a 1941 birthday so that's about nine years over there before he was born. Were those her teaching years? I'm intrigued. When I once confessed to Gran I wanted to train to be a teacher, just like her, she looked at me with a sad expression and said, 'Don't use me as your model, Sally. My path was not smooth.'

That's the only clue I have to a mystery. I should be able to yield some answers. I did teach, gave it up to write. It was appropriate; my boys were growing up and two together was a handful while James was so often out of the state and even of the country with his army. Writers wanting to write well need to research; research takes up a lot of time. So I left work to be more with the boys and use the time at home to write. It worked well.

So, is that relevant? Not. Tantalising cues? Again, not. Yet the more I think about certainties, the more questions they seem to prompt. If researching Katherine's papers yields some intrigue, then I'll have the essence of a romance or a mystery, something to pursue. These notes of Gran's are a start.

I look at Mog, staring at me with his big eyes. Kittens and balls of wool come to mind. It's for me to do some untangling!

I gaze out of the window. We have a hot and dry summer forecast ahead of us for 2018. Today's November warmth is nothing like it will be in January or February; already the garden's looking dry. I drift or daydream, whatever it's now called, and try to visualise wartime London after the bombings. Yet that's my mother's history – herstory as I once quipped. Her story obviously links with Dad's, and Dad's should link with hers. It's something like those ancestry chases on TV. I turn on my recorder.

Mum has flashbacks, most often of a vivid few moments as she watches a young boy crying angrily while his hair was being clipped short in front of a kitchen fire. This flashes onto her mind's eye so vividly she hears, spoken crossly, the words 'Oh, Roger.' She remembers how the black metal fire surround glowed a gloriously vivid red and orange when it was warm and she was not allowed to touch it. I remember how acutely sad I was when she mentioned how she wishes her flashbacks would show her the face that belongs to the voice. 'I'm sure it was my mother's but I can't really remember.' So sad.

Mog stirred on my lap. 'You know, Mr Cat's Whiskers, you should go back into the laundry. I've work to do. Mum's is quite a story really. She knows even less of her father; just that he was in the navy and blown up at sea by a submarine. Her parents' marriage records were included amongst the thousands burned in the Blitz, as she referred to it; her father was listed as a 'manager'. I didn't know of what but it indicated a creditable level of education and character, as I said to her. After the bombing – she once mentioned 1949 but would never talk to me about it – she came over to Australia with a bunch of other kids from the home. They came on a ship called the *Ormonde*. They were just sent. All she would tell me was 'this is a country built on immigration and there was nothing unusual in my coming. I was only one of hundreds, maybe thousands of children.'

My dad once told me, when I was pestering him for more detail about Mum's story, that many of her friends had grown up thinking their parents were dead yet they weren't. He recounted a tale horrible to my young ears. I pestered Dad for answers. It seemed authorities had taken it upon themselves to decide that bombed-out British industrial cities were not places for homeless children. About 130,000 children from four to fourteen were sent out to Australia – and Canada as well – 'to have a happy healthy life in a new country', he said. Supposedly they were all orphans; they had all been in care in Britain.

I was stroking Mog, for my own reassurance. 'You know, Mog, the word was that the countries wanted good British stock to increase a future population. There are words for that statement, unpleasant ones. You know, Mog-Whiskers, even you are loved more than they were, back then.'

Dad told me how Mum had been very unhappy in the orphanage after she arrived, so much so she hated talking about it. Armed with a psychological component in my own degree, I tried one afternoon to ease out a few answers but all she would tell me was that her experiences there turned her off religion. I do know that when Dad realised how worried she was about not knowing all her past, he encouraged her to make enquiries which ultimately allowed her to read some old records held in England. I was able to do that for her and I found her family name was Bell, the surname found on her father's rental records. They named him as Ernest, her mother as Vera and her older brother as Roger. She discovered she'd been registered as Eleanor. She chose to stay as Emily.

I traced those records and managed even a few email responses from grandchildren of others, who, like Mum, were long thought to have died post-war in Britain. I hadn't been able to find any of Mum's relatives. I had been horrified to know how various governments and authorities had simply written off the transported children, even in many cases informing their families years ago that they had died. To think a child had died was sadness enough, but to be deliberately kept unaware that these little sons, daughters and cousins were actually in orphanages on the other side of the world; that they were being denied an education, trained only as labourers or domestic workers and enduring cruelties and abuse in many cases, thinking they were truly orphaned, I found almost too appalling to be true. Yet the tales were – are – factual.

Granny Kath was still alive when that film called *The Leaving of Liverpool* was first shown on TV. I watched it at a later showing and I remember incidents and investigations being reported in the newspapers. I found it hard to accept that my own mum was also a victim of such injustice, such cruelty. I hope that in reading my version of her story I was able to give Mum a more balanced acceptance of what was and what is now. Yet she persists in this idea of Granny Kath having a hidden secret.

I tickled Mog under his chin and his purring became a rumble to register decibels. I had to grin. 'You know, Mr Cat, my mum and Gran were a good match for each other. I'd call them both strong women, as Dad described. Mum may not have been into religion but she drove Gran to church most weeks despite what prejudices of her own she had to cope with and that's where Gran died.'

It was in 2011, first Sunday in Advent – a date Mum then said would please her. Gran just failed to wake up after one of the hymns at church. Mum was singing and noticed Gran's voice fade away but assumed she was relaxing into her favourite spot on the pew; she no longer stood up to sing. I remember the date, 27 November, and Gran would have been 98 at Christmas. Mum always drove Granny Kath to the Lutheran church, but after Gran died, I don't think Mum ever went again. When I suggested it once, she said she went off religion years ago but Gran needed absolution. I was intrigued and admired her persistence in escorting Gran even though she herself had no loyalty to the doctrine.

Mog's now actually snoring on my lap! I have to grin. 'Come on, you fat bundle of whiskers, into the laundry with you.'

He slips from my grasp and lands on a couple of fallen papers, his claw hooking up a corner. I pull to dislodge it and there's a date…and a number of pages, notebook style. Just a quick peek…

I bundle Mog back into the laundry and kneel down by the fallen papers. I can see a date, written boldly. *So what or when are you looking for, Sally?*

Have to start somewhere. I turn on my recorder. Katherine's words, plenty of space for them. This is dated 1929 – nearly a century ago and Gran was actually there, wherever 'there' might be. Perhaps I'll read the dates aloud.

Katherine

4

4 October 1929

'Hello, this is Katherine speaking. May I…'

'I want Miss Symonds, if she's there.' Imperious, even rude. Has to be one of those Mr Taits.

'ROSIE!'

She clip-clopped up to me in her ballet slippers and pushed past, making an exaggerated moue to me as she snatched the receiver. I moued back, left her to it and escaped to the little box room. It'd been my haven for these last two weeks in Melbourne, but it was now time to pack my things.

And that telephone! I think it's living with Gran'mama Beatrice for so long that renders it both friend and enemy to Rosalie. If ever someone was superstitious – and suspicious – of the telephone, it was Gran'mama Beatrice. My mother, her daughter, is just as bad!

I pulled my shoes from under the bed. This dislike of the telephone started when one of my uncles telephoned Mama to tell her of Gran'mama Beatrice being killed while she was out riding. Rosalie was there at the time, not me. It seems to me that's when the family suspicion was born, about the telephone only bringing the worst kind of news. Here in Melbourne of course, with her waiting to hear about some career prospects, quite different.

I lifted my suitcase out too. Anything else under this bed? Seems not. It's been fun staying here in Melbourne, the shows and things, but now it's definitely time to go home. I like Rosie well enough, and she's my cousin – if that's relative (ha ha), because the only thing we share, really and truly in our hearts, is that long-dead Gran'mama. In anything else, we are poles apart. Oh yoicks, I'll never close the lid on this old suitcase. Oh here she comes. Trouble…

'Oh, Katherine! Why couldn't you have been quicker on the uptake? He wasn't so helpful today. And do refer to me by my proper name on the telephone, in future, PLEASE.' She plonked onto my bed, careless about my pile of stockings, and started picking at the candlewick cover.

I pulled my things from under her. 'Uptake? Another word you've borrowed from those American people at the great JC Williamson's lot, no doubt. Honestly, you are so bossy at times, Rosalee-ee-ee Jane Symonds. And do you really think JayCee remembers everyone in the choruses? It's only a few weeks since they were welcoming the great Pavlova again. Be honest, Rosalie, you are a good dancer, but…well, hardly in the same league! You dress up in Hollandia costumes and it's a wonder you don't have to dance in, wha'dya'call'ems – *sabots*! It's not exactly ballet in the Green Mill and your dancing is ballroom stuff with strange men.' Maybe I wasn't being kind.

She glowered and aimed my pillow at me. 'Katherine Flack, you're horrible! You met Mr Matear from the Green Mill, didn't you? That friend of Gran'pa who gave me a chance with his dancers? Mr Tom Carlyon is the other owner/director and they're both respectable gentlemen.' She slithered over to sit on the end of my bed. 'Now listen to this: Mr John Tait from His Majesty's has told Mr Carlyon he has his eye on me.'

I plonked onto the blanket box. I'd heard it all before. Captive audience, me. No option but to hear it again.

'Don't raise your eyebrows at me, Katherine. Yes, that was Mr John Tait on the telephone. And do understand, little cousin, the Mill is known as a high-class dance hall throughout all of Melbourne. It's perfectly respectable. My Gran'pa Smythe approves and I'm sure our Gran'mama Beatrice would too. I was only a toddler when she said I posed like a dancer and Aunt Esther, your own mum, reminded me of that. And I know I'm good.'

She rang her fingers through her thick brown hair and thrust out her chin. I so dislike that habit of hers, and then she'll speak at me with her eyes closed. Haughty habit – Mum says she's inherited it from her mother, Lilian. Here comes the lecture – yep, eyes flickering under her lashes…

'Katherine, you couldn't know, coming from Adelaide, that here in St Kilda is where all the best people come for entertainment, as Mr Carlyon says. He's involved with JC Limited, knows the Taits quite well – of course – and the firm knows my worth. The Tait brothers are actually managing directors of JayCees with Mr George Tallis, and their opinion is important, Katherine, to anyone like me who wants to be noticed. Mr Tait likes my dancing. He told Mr Carlyon so. I know the moves, I know the steps and I love to feel I can also express my own feelings at times. And we are allowed to improvise in demonstrations; unless we have a structured dance, with its own steps, to show the client dancers. And you, with your religious upbringing, you think less of me for it. Admit…'

'Rosie! That's rubbish and you know it.'

'Oh, all right. but you don't understand. If I tell you that Mr Tait, Mr John Tait, has musical theatre in his sights, so he said, no doubt you'll think me totally immoral. but it's perfectly acceptable, Kath.'

So I'm cousin Kath again…

'He wants only the tasteful acts to attract the best people. I believe he has ambitions to be a Melbourne Mr Gilbert, or Mr Sullivan, with shows like *Pinafore* – I know you like that one! The original JC company brought those English shows to Melbourne and the other cities as well. They're musical theatre, not music hall, and that's what Mr John wants. He *is* ambitious but says he'll hasten slowly. He calls me and Jennifer and Emily – you met them – his three prospects. He and his brothers have big interests in films, in London as well. It's so exciting, Kath, just thinking what I might be able to do!'

Oh my, know it off by heart… I stood up to resume my packing.

She leaned to catch my arm. 'Don't you turn your nose up at me, Kath. I thought you would understand, you! No one else is interested. It's dancing and oh, I want to dance! I have to!'

I gave up and sat down next to her. Can't say I'm all that interested but dancing is her passion, best to let her talk, to hear her out. 'Rosie. I may be younger than you but I do understand how you feel. I have ambitions too. Ambition can burn, Rosie, I know it. For instance, I want to write, and write and write, but I still have another year at school to tolerate. Not easy.'

'Not the same, Kath. Your father's happy with what you want to do, isn't he? Mine's always criticising me. If I finished school, it would've pleased him but I wasn't ever going to gain a university place. Nor did I want to. I'm nearly nineteen and here they treat me like a woman of the world and not just a farmer's daughter.'

I thought that a silly remark. 'Rosalee! Uncle George is hardly just a farmer. But I know what you mean. I'm the eldest daughter and everyone says I'll be such a help to my mother. That's not my role in life either, much as I love Mum. I want to be a teacher eventually.'

'I know you do. I do care, but…' She sighed. 'If Mum were still here… Did you know my Aunt Faith's husband caught the Spanish influenza at the same time as Mum and Gran'ma Smythe? Gran'pa Smythe said he took a while to die. Ghastly way to go…' She shuddered. 'My mother would stand up for me, I know, if… I so miss her, Kath. It makes me feel ill when I think how she died. She's missed years of me and how I wish she could see me, now. She would have understood and persuaded my father to let me dance. I will do it, and for her. I will be famous one day.'

She stood upright, arms above her head with her fingers delicately posing and ankles crossed. Must she always pose? Everything is extreme with Rosie; she even talks in capital letters.

As if on cue, she reached over. 'Oh…here, have some grapes. You know, it's not only dancing, it's the whole lifestyle here in Melbourne. It's fast, it's fashion and all about being ready for the next opportunity. It's the modern way. Mr John – Tait, that is – says it won't be long before it's all films now. He says we must move with the times. That includes eventually taking control of the firm, so rumours have it, and

Mr Tallis is up for a knighthood. If he becomes Sir George – imagine that! Then he's expected to retire and the Taits will take over control of the JCW firm. So Mr Tait is important to me, you see? It'll soon be 1930 and already they've started giving awards to the best film stars – remember Janet Gaynor a few months ago? She was the first actress to win one. I went to see the film – you know, *Seventh Heaven* – with Aunt Faith. It was lovely and she's so tiny.' She laughed. 'Janet Gaynor, not my Aunt Faith! If I make the grade, and I have the looks, or so says Mr John, I may even try for the films!'

I was growing tired of all this obscure theatre stuff. 'C'mon, Rosie, let's go have a cup of cocoa. It's pouring outside and listen to that wind! Real Melbourne weather. Cocoa sounds good.'

Rosie was lost in her own thoughts.

I flicked her arm. 'Rosalie Jane Symonds! If wishes were fishes… Look here, did I tell you my mother went to see Pavlova? She went with Lucille, that's Uncle William's head of chambers' wife. It was at the Theatre Royal, in Adelaide of course, and…'

That raised her eyebrows. 'Yes, Pavlova went there after here, I remember. Oh, how blissful to see her dance. She's poetry in motion. Gran'pa Smythe took me, a few weeks ago. I saw her in *Autumn Leaves*. She played the last chrysanthemum. You know, Pavlova creates her own choreography. She styled that dance to Chopin for *Autumn Leaves*, and I knew – because your mother told me once – that Chopin was one of our Gran'ma Beatrice's favourite composers. Oh, if I close my eyes…'

'Rosie, for heaven's sake! I know I live in a country town without a theatre but I do know what choreography is. And Mum likes to play Chopin too, just like her mother did, and even I can play some of his music, though not all the tricky bits. Here's something else: Anna Pavlova drove to Hahndorf, well, she calls it Ambleside, to see Mister Heysen at his home, The Cedars. It's no big city, Rosie, but it's my home town and Mum told me there was quite a buzz of excitement around the shops. She was so pleased she actually telephoned me. So… how's that? He's the artist, you know, Hans Heysen, world-famous.

Mum told me Pavlova bought a painting from him, or wanted to and he wouldn't sell the one she liked but offered to make her another and send it on to her. So how wonderful is that? Two world-famous people knowing each other, who live a whole world apart and then meet up in my little town! My auntie Evelyn knows him well because of her painting of course, and Opa knew Mr Heysen well, too. He came to Opa's funeral.'

Rosalie sat upright at that. 'I wish I'd met him, you know, your other Gran'pa, your Opa. Never did. And I haven't even been to your house, have I, yet you've been to mine at Cumquats. You've met my Gran'pa Smythe – obviously, because he lives here – in this house! I do remember your Opa dying. I was there when your mother, Aunt Esther, came to Cumquats to see Gran'ma Beatrice's grave; it was her birthday or something and the phone call came. Pa said Aunt Esther was upset enough that day remembering Gran'ma Beatrice and she was only just brightening up a bit – talking to my handsome brothers of course – when the telephone rang. Pa was upset because she was. For your mother to have that news of Opa dying, knowing she'd worry about Uncle Frank, on top of the way she was feeling already, well, that's why Pa drove her all the way home through Adelaide in the Talbot.'

'Yes, I think it was that call that started the whole telephone hatred thing with my mum. She'd always grumbled about her mother blaming the telephone for all the bad news, and that call gave her the horrors, well and truly. She knew my papa would absolutely disintegrate at Opa's death. Since that call, she's grown even more superstitious of the telephone, calling it a harbinger of unhappiness. Poor Mama. And Opa – I wish you had met him, Rosie. He was truly, really German – to his bootstraps, my dad says. Mama calls us a diverse family, a blending of cultures. She always has the right word for something, my mother. Can't forget she once taught English in a Melbourne girls' school.'

Rosie was doing arm movements but that stopped her short. 'Oh! I didn't know that, Kath. Truly? Here in Melbourne?'

'Yes. She calls Melbourne her second-best favourite city after Adelaide but Hahndorf is her most favourite place of all. Did you know that my Oma Kate – I was called after her – often tells me stories of what she and Gran'mama Beatrice used to do when they were best friends together and before they married. Oma Kate became Frau Herbert Flach and our Gran'mama Beatrice married Gran'papa Arthur Symonds in the same year – many months apart. In fact, my dad was born the very day they married. He's a twin, you know.

'You know, Rosie, if she hadn't been so keen on riding, our Gran'mama Beatrice would still be with us. How awful to have a horse roll on top of you… And hey! Stop pulling the threads on that bedspread. You'll have your Aunt Faith chasing after me, 'cos it's on my bed!'

I stretched my arms and rubbed my hands. Hers were poised above her head, delicate finger placements again. Thinks she's the dying swan, honestly. She was upright now, ballet-clad feet pinkly placed at right angles – wonder she doesn't tip over. I stared at her. Was she listening or daydreaming again? She's just so precious in her attitudes; she strikes a pose at the end of every sentence.

I don't know what chores she has to do at home but she's hopeless at darning her stockings and when I told her of a hole in her heel she said, 'Oh, it doesn't matter. No one looks at the back of your heels.' So I darned her pink lacy ones for her and she didn't even say thank you. And she doesn't clean off the iron before pressing her collars and she left a burn mark on hers and took one of mine!

Nor does she say much that's nice about her Aunt Faith, who lives here in this house. Calls her fat and and says she smells under her arms when she hugs. So self-centred.

Sally

5

5 November 2017, later in the day

Wow! I sit back, realising the day is well advanced. What a long spiel! No mere diary entry, it's long and not easy to sort out in my head. What detail in the narration! So this cousin Rosalie I'd barely heard of wants to be a ballet dancer. And there's significant background to Dad's family tree. Strange. Even for a writer, and sometime historical researcher as I am, it isn't easy refocusing on the here and now after reading of the past. This suitcase page is almost too much to take in; too many people. It may have been Katherine's life but I need time to absorb it all.

My brain's still out of sync. When Mum arrived with all this, I was drafting a commission not at all related to this time travelling – a wine grower's report for which I'll be well paid. If I complete it on time! Prioritise, Sally, prioritise. Might as well regroup. Other things waiting for me, and a twingeing broken tooth I need to have fixed. Best concentrate on the present, the here and now.

No doubt, this is intriguing stuff – looks like an entire writing pad or notebook…oh goodness, it's still her same day too. Recorder on…

Katherine

6

4 October 1929, later

Rosie was in a real talkative mood but all her talk is of herself, or so it seems to me; it all relates to her anyway. I think I went on to say that we'd both had pain in our lives.

'And you know, Rosalie, I could write a book… Opa died of a stroke, like Gran'pa Symonds. Just toppled over, so my dad said. He was there at the time and so was Uncle Josh. Dad said Oma was quite stoic. She wasn't German but she's always been Oma Kate. She cried a lot with my mum but said Opa was quite worn out after the war and anyway, he was nearly eighty. Aunt Evie has always lived with them, which is specially good for Oma now, so she's not alone. And she doesn't go away painting much now – Evie, that is. She says she's heading for her fifties and it's time to take things more quietly. You know, she and I have the same birthday, on Christmas Day! She'll never stop painting, though, and she's quite famous.'

Rosalie was posing again, her arms outstretched, her fingers delicately poised. 'Yes, I do know that, Kath – you've told me so many times. Your doctor Elena sent a picture of hers to Erica for a present and I've seen it. And Ralph keeps me up to date with what he does and some news of your family. He talks about a lot of things in his letters, but do you see much of his carving? He says he likes capturing wild animals in their movements. Capturing is a funny word to use, though, no?'

'That's just Ralph. Ambiguity is his fashion – plays games with words. He's always whittling. You know, it's a bit odd you and Ralph being friends, Rosie. My mother told me she and our papa used to write long letters to each other. That was when she was teaching in

Melbourne and then – did you know he actually proposed to her in a letter?'

'Oh, how romantic! But hey, don't imagine your brother and I are doing the same. I like him, but he's too young for me, Kath. Nor does he like music or dancing or theatre. He wrote, saying dancing is a form of exhibitionism when it's performed publicly, out of the home and for other people. We do not agree on that point!'

I laughed at that. 'Sounds like Ralph. For a brother he's all right – bit bossy at times but works hard. He sees the business as his future. He loves the smell of timber when it's being cut, he says, and Papa always says the same. Left school as soon as he could. But I can't imagine Ralph writing letters. That does surprise me.'

I moved to close my suitcase with a decided click. Enough talking. 'C'mon, Rosie. I've done for now. Hot drink or cold? I know what you like – let's go have a Cottees. That's if there's any Passiona left. I love that flavour.'

She was already at the door then turned. 'Kath, why is your name on your suitcase F L A C K? Thought your name was Flach – with an "h".'

'Our name was Flach once but Dad changed it to Flack before the war, when it wasn't popular to be of German blood. But he's very proud of the family business and what Opa built up. Hahndorf has lots of people who came from his father's country. I'm proud of them – most of them anyway. Our doctor Elena – she's Mama's good friend – well, she comes from yet another country. I thought it was Poland but when I said that once, she gave me a silly laugh and said she wished it was! It's somewhere over there, anyway. Doc Elena encouraged my cousin Susannah into medicine and she's now a medical researcher into strokes and things like that. She's quite famous in medical circles – she's older of course. Mum says she went to Cumquats one time when I was a baby but you may not remember her.'

Rosie was too busy digging in the icebox to listen. 'You know, Kath, this ice keeps drinks really chilly, and the butter and stuff. Good enough for me and my Gran'pa Smythe but Mr Carlyon at the Mill has been talking about a new Kelvinator refrigerator machine that comes from America. Have you heard of it? It uses electricity to keep things cooler, even frozen. I'm not sure how they work. Gran'pa says the iceman's never let him down and things stay cool enough in here.'

I'd already filched my Passiona from its depths. 'I do so agree, Rosalie. My arm froze after only a few seconds in there! You know, I hope you'll come and visit us. Hahndorf is so pretty and Ralph of course would love to see you again. Arthur's learning to work in the business too – he's Jacinta's twin and they're only just fourteen and I don't know what he wants to do. Jacinta says she'll make up her own mind but I've no idea if she has plans. Mama's description is a good one – diverse. Seems like so many of us now and we're all different, aren't we, all of us cousins? Me, I'm almost sixteen and if I'm not careful, Dad'll be asking me to work in his office or something. No. No way. That's not for me. I want to write a book and finish it before I start university. I've always wanted to be a teacher. My choice.'

So it all ended better than it started; we straightened out all the family connections.

Then the telephone rang again! Rosalie jumped up to answer and I watched her face as she talked and listened. She seemed really pleased with what was being arranged. I know my mother will be pleased that we've had these two weeks together; she believes in family bonding – her phrase. Nevertheless, tomorrow I'm heading home and truthfully it's not too soon. We're too different, Rosalie and me, to be real friends, but I suppose we've enjoyed getting to know each other better this fortnight. I like the way she calls her parents Mum and Dad, though, shorter, easier to say. And Gran'pa not Gran'papa, Gran'ma without all the mama's saves time.

So, an early start for the Adelaide train, then overnight at Uncle William's little house – his town house, he calls it, then next day, the train to Bridgewater and home. I'm not really sorry. It'll be good to catch up with Dottie, who likes to be called Dorothy now, and the other girls at Tognarelli's café. They'll want to hear all about Melbourne.

Sally

7

Friday, 30 March 2018

Oh wow! Time has flown by and I've been busy with other things. Can't ignore family responsibilities, not even writers! Katherine writes as if it's a novel, not just a journal entry. She's economical with paper, though, no lavish margins, no indents. Haven't uncovered any spicy mysteries yet for Mum to enjoy. I've just done a speedy reread, needed to refresh. Must focus.

My own life intervened. To recap: things have happened *for* me and *to* me, such as Christmas, then my birthday and various family events and, not least, my James home on a few weeks post-tour leave. He was in the army when we met; he's a career officer, and popular within his regiment, which is good. I'm feeling quite old, but being fifty-five is more acceptable than turning fifty-six. That extra number would indicate that I'm turning the corner into the middle of middle-aged.

I need that focus. James is now back in Darwin, I drove him to the airport this morning and today our boys are somewhere with mates, no doubt planning some upcoming weekend shenanigans. I've not been totally idle; another article for the *Wine Growers* is away in the mail, I've completed a polemic for a literary magazine, actually submitted to a couple of poetry magazines, and had some riddles accepted by the *NSW Education Magazine*, so my writing conscience is clear. All very twenty-first century stuff; normality.

For late March it's sultry but cloudy and I feel there's a change in the wind. However, I've picked up the suitcase again from the spare room, where it spent most of the recent weeks, neglected, and I'm now lounging with a drink out on the veranda, Mog warming the cushion on the other chair. The last pages I read weeks ago are waiting on the top of the pile, clips around those I've read. Do I have a new approach niggling at me? Is anything jumping out at me from Katherine's notes? It'll be hard work sinking into the book again but today I'm all alone; time to think…

What does strike me as strange is that even though she wrote these pages almost ninety years ago, Granny Katherine as a young girl sounds like any young girl of now. Well, the language is perhaps a bit stuffier, or more precise than we use now, yet I'm relating to her; that is quite paradoxical, almost baffling. I'm linking the young girl with the elderly lady I knew more recently, Granny Kath of the sweetest smile and still mischievous eye and also the beautifully thick whiteish hair tied back in a chignon. And those lavender-coloured cardigans! Mum told me once how Granny Kath boasted once she was considered a beauty in her day with 'silver gold hair that hung in natural waves over her shoulders'. When I visited her, I know she liked me to brush it for her – a hundred strokes. I don't know who did the brushing when I wasn't there. Dad said it was her one great vanity.

But Katherine's account here in my hands is a fantastic pulling together of names and people. Granny Katherine was one of the Hahndorf branch of the Flack, aka Flach, family. I feel a real pull of sentiment as I gently trace my fingers over the name etched into the lid of the old suitcase. Gran married David Downham in 1934 and my dad was their only child – to my knowledge! He was Samuel Francis and died of cancer back in 2012 not long after Granny died. So, relatively recent history.

Granny Kath almost scored a century. She'd declared her love for writing and it's so – what's the word? – fluent. She has – had – a gift, no doubting it. Her voice sings out to me. Wow!

I move indoors. The evening mozzies are making their presence felt. Coffee is called for; don't feel like a meal, though. Slice of toast and honey sounds appealing. I'll take a quick peek at the pile of those papers. Just the ones on top…

Ahah, a page torn roughly from a notebook; ruled lines. Just a short account: Katherine's mother Esther Flach had put a loaf into the oven for too long. So real and lively, the little report, I swear I can smell the smoke.

Oh no! Sally Olsen! You're a fool! Burnt toast again – well, coffee will do.

I riffle through under the lower layers of paper. No more photographs yet but there is a touch of the mysteries – saw the name Avril, for instance. I have a certain feeling it's no doll on that photo. Hmm. I do have a half-formulated plot to link in if possible and suddenly recall one of my lecturer's favourite sayings about fiction – or faction, as she claimed it to be. 'Have a go. Not hocus pocus but focus locus.' We in the class translated that as meaning well grounded intelligence. I settle down on the sofa, and place the box between my feet. Mog reclines at the other end, his eyes narrowed as he watches.

It's darkening outside, a few heavenly rumbles indicating the possibility of a storm overnight. I actually decided to heat some leftovers for my tea and put Mog in the laundry for his own meal. Now, wine in hand, I'm still undecided about this Granny Kath material. It's an almighty muddle of names. For a book, too many; need to drop most of them and focus on one.

Now, what's this? I'll read and record for James…

'This' is a short note, untidy pen work but with a date, Tuesday 1 October 1929. Almost ninety years ago. It's a report by Katherine about a note from Jacinta's school. She was the young sister, a twin, I think – twins are everywhere in this family! I don't remember Granny speaking of her… Seems that Jacinta had to stop her petition and fund-raising around the school; that if she did not promise to do so, she would be reported to the police as it was 'gaining money under duress' and some parents protested. Hm, proactive is this sister. Katherine has written more fully…

Mum is livid and is going to see the school tomorrow. It seems that Jazz is quite despairing of the decree in Victoria – and our parliament seems to like it – that wild kangaroos be culled as there are too many and they are eating the grass intended for the sheep and cattle. The farmers are petitioning the chief secretary to declare an open season on the kangaroos. Jazz apparently has written on her petition that monies collected will be used to buy hay for the farmer's animals so they will leave the wild ones alone 'and in their natural environment which was theirs long before European settlement tried to take it away from them'. I admire her zeal if not her logic. Don't know if Mum is angry with the school or with Jazz! I rather admire Jazz for fighting against what she feels is wrong. Mum has long declared 'Jacinta has a social conscience.' Guess this is an example of what's to come.

Untidy handwriting and not much has changed in schools either. I remember some notes my boys brought home. Also, I like the name Jazz: it brings her alive, real! At the time of Katherine's writing, jazz music was all the rage – loved by some and deplored by many. Ahah, here's a page of plain notepaper dated…erm…a year later. Time obviously passes for Katherine, too. This looks like another long epistle, and typewritten. A bonus!

I demolish the leftovers and sit back to sip my wine; it's a smooth shiraz – McLaren Vale, this one…delightful.

Katherine

8

7 December 1930

Things are starting to happen so I decided to keep a journal to remember. For a start, it's so hot today, Mum says her thermometer says 110 degrees. Rosalie will be here at Hahndorf on the 10th, Wednesday. She'll love my little home town, I'm sure. As long as she keeps her flirty eyes away from Kris – she had a lot of experience batting her eyelashes at men at that Windmill place and then dancing and high kicking in the chorus line there. She's been there for over a year now. I know Ralph wasn't pleased to hear about that.

But Kris – that's Kristoffer Schmidt – thinks it's a lark, Huh. He and I are a pair – a team, he calls it – and we've been that way for a few months now. I think Ralph would really prefer Kris to like Rosalie instead of me. He told me that Kris can be a little fast and needed a girl who's done some living to keep him under control. I took exception to that. I am not a silly child any longer. That my brother can speak so critically of one of his closest friends yet still welcome his company is hypocrisy of the first order; he's so uppity now that he's chosen religion. But it *is* pleasant of Uncle William to bring Rosalie to stay for Christmas and all is growing festive. Even little Alicia is coming, because her school has finished for the year and she wants to be with her Papa as much as possible. Lovely of Aunt Erica to allow that (though I know she's so busy running her medical practice now).

I do hope Rosie isn't too depressed about everything. More cheerfully, I, Katherine Beatrice Flack, completed my last school exam yesterday! It was German. I did well at mathematics too, big surprise! I am so pleased to have finished but now I have to wait to see if I can apply to the teachers college. And Mum wants me to wait a year, till

I'm eighteen. She says I'm too young for such a responsible career and deserve some time learning all about myself! What on earth does she mean? Not always good sharing a birthday with Christmas, but when I'm seventeen, perhaps they'll stop treating me like a child.

Now it's a whole week later!

Goodness, what a string of exclamation marks in my last entry. I'm happier with the typewriting but I do need to practise. Carbon paper is rather expensive – threepence a sheet. I haven't written much in my journals this last year, too much hard study, but I think I've done well enough to gain a place in college. Classes don't start till March next year. Kris congratulated me as I walked home yesterday and we're going to a quiz in his church hall tonight. Last time, we won! He's organised his friend Rauf to accompany Rosalie. I enjoy these quizzes and Kris is good to be seen with – soooooo good-looking. Dorothy likes him too. Well, she can look elsewhere!

Rosalie's broken ankle is recovered enough for walking and she has to keep it moving, but she cannot now do too much of the ballet dancing. Strangely, she seems quite optimistic and confesses to me that films are still an option. Oh my! Admittedly, she is beautiful with her rich brown hair. It has auburn highlights, quite glorious, but she professes to prefer my pale gold colour and I let mine grow and hers is still only shoulder-length, because she likes it bobbed. The style is named after a man's hairstyle and indeed some of the girls have it almost shaven at the sides. Wonder who Bob was? Must admit, they're usually the thespian types or, as Mum calls them, soroptimists. Rosalie favours all those dresses that fall in a straight line over her slim shape. Quite short too, some of them. Mum tells me I'm too curvy for that style and should be thankful.

Ralph admires Rosalie but can be critical of her; considers her rather fast. He speaks of her to me as if he's already a pastor in the church. I do believe that's become his main ambition. He's becoming a bit of a pain as a brother – he's only a few months older than me but throws his weight around as far as I and the twins are concerned. I'm glad I can write all this in your pages, journal, because I cannot, dare not, say much to anyone else. Mum and Dad think the sun shines from his blue-grey eyes. Heaven only knows how he'll fit in all the study with his love of the business. I wonder how Dad thinks of the idea? I know he's always talked of Ralph following him in the business. But then, Dad left Opa's business, didn't he, to build this one? I'm beginning to think Ralph might be feeling a bit restless in some ways, though, as if he'd like to broaden his own horizons (excuse the cliché). And he is eighteen, old enough to make up his mind. Big and burly enough too. Whatever he thinks of Rosie, he certainly enjoys speaking with her. He's my brother but I haven't ever been such friends as he is with her. He listens intently to her gossipy stories – and she has a few to tell!

She likes talking to Mum, or Aunt Esther as she calls her quite properly, and I think it's because she misses her own mother. Mum quite likes being called Mum instead of Mama too – that's what I changed to after Melbourne. She enjoys chatting with Rosie too, actually calls her circumspect (one of her words) and I'm the gossipy one in her eyes. When I hinted Ralph likes Rosie, that he gives her those certain looks, Mum looked at me like I was dirt on her shoe.

'Really, Katherine Beatrice, it's silly to even speculate. Personalities aside, they're first cousins. Besides which, it's no small decision your brother will be making if he does undertake pastoral studies. He will be required to have a wife who is of the Lutheran Church.'

Of course I argued. 'Mum, they're always sitting outside on the big log seat, chatting. She poses and throws out her chest and tosses her hair. She can't resist flirting. She's quite a political animal, you know, and knows some people who influence the Victorian parliament and they argue about politics. Those people from the JC Williamson group gave some weird parties and she met lots of them at such events. She's all right, but awfully single-minded. All I had from her every hour of every day was dancing, dancing, dancing. I do feel sorry for her now, wondering if her ankle will ever be strong enough. But I can put up with her, Mum, just, because she really likes our house now she's seen it and raves on about the new rooms, the dragon on the stairwell and the carving on the beams that Dad and Ralph did.'

Mum signalled for me to sit down at the table and lifted the kettle off the hob. That was her way of saying she'd like a 'talk'. Oh dear. She poured us both a coffee.

'Mum, Rosie's rather condescending to Alicia and I think that's a mistake. Alicia is only a child, not eleven until next May. Doc Elena likes her, says she's – what was it? Oh yes – strangely canny but with a pleasant nature. Doc Elena writes to Aunt Erica, as you know, not only because they're both doctors, an' she gives me snippets of what goes on at Cumquats. Seems Rosalie's brothers adore Alicia. Doc Elena says Aunt Erica thinks Alicia is a future prime minister. Hah. Well, she *is* her daughter, I suppose. I think she's Uncle William's favourite but Aunt Erica dotes on their two boys, Steve and Nick. They visited Melbourne when I was with Rosie last year, you know, and her Gran'pa Smythe let them stay in his attic bedrooms. He's nice.'

She sensed I was on my soapbox – her phrase – and was waiting for more. She wasn't disappointed. It's so good to have this time to be just Mum and me. Don't have much chance. And I am grown-up now and not a schoolgirl any more.

'You know, Mum, boys have the lot, don't they? Special schools, special treatment – they're made to feel special. He's taking his boys over to England to start school over there, but because Aunt Erica was ill they postponed their trip from last August and so the boys have to start a term late. They have different terms in England. I asked Uncle William why he wanted to send the boys away but he says he spent some schooling years at the Windermere school and wants his boys to have the same chances. It'll cost thousands of pounds, Mum...'

'Katherine, my dear, it is unfortunately the way of the world and, common sense or not, my brother William is a successful Adelaide lawyer, high in the chambers, and makes the money. More importantly, he really loved that school and says it gave him a good grounding for Oxford. I don't think he's aiming that high for Stephen and Nicholas, but he's quite canny in a financial way, you know. He owns that house in Kendal. It's not far from the school at all, only five or six miles on a good road. You see, the Wall Street crash last October affected some of his investments but not as badly as it could have done – he's quite astute is your Uncle William. However, he has secured sailings at a reasonable price, only £38! That's for each, of course. I know all about that trip – he's asked my opinion. There are a few extra charges but that's certainly not expensive for more than a month on a ship – all meals and accommodation as well.'

She picked up a sock of Dad's that needed darning. 'As for females in this world, Katherine, there are now opportunities I never had. I often wonder what some of the young ladies I taught at that rather exclusive Melbourne girls' school made of their lives.' She lifted up her darning with a wry grin. No words were needed.

'Your Gran'papa Symonds was very forward-looking when I decided to leave my career to marry your dad. They both took some convincing but did acknowledge I had thought things through. That's what you must do, Kathy, and you'll have my support as much as I can give it. You have to aim high yourself. And, oh goodness gracious, now I have your own little sister Jacinta wanting to be an environmental scientist, or a botanist. And Arthur, he seems to want to be an artist! Oh my.' She sighed, put her darning on that table and sat back, looking at me. With a sense of purpose.

Oh no! I know what's coming – this is why I was invited to share a cup with her.

'In reality, Katherine dear, all you need is to find a sensible occupation for a year then you can embark on your own chosen career. Why not work with me here, do our office accounts and the ordering. I would love to have help with that. For only next year?'

'Oh, Mother! Same old story. Stop nagging me about my duty, do!' I nearly slammed the door when I went out but decided that was a bit childish. I'm no longer that child and Kris does agree with that. But my mother never gives up wanting me to be in her mould.

Sally

9

Extremely late on Sunday, 1 April 2018

Not sure when I start and stop recording, better more than less, I feel, although no doubt I'm mentioning chats with the cat and sips of shiraz now and again – listener, enjoy! I must try to flick the thing off when it's not relevant. Only a couple of days ago for me in present times; weeks for Katherine. All this time zone stuff. Wow!

Cracking thunderstorm here in our north-eastern suburbs of Adelaide; no point going to bed and sleeping. Hoping for rain but not a whisper of it yet. My boys are home and apparently enjoying a game of cards in the family room. They are really good friends – but they are twins! We relate well; it's much less confrontational now they are adults. They tolerate their mother and her hours locked away on the keyboard – a routine that suits us all when their father is away. All so much more amicable than when they were in their teens and – even worse – oh, those awful uni years!

So, back to my grandmother. Parental conflict with young adults is no new phenomenon! Young Katherine is not the conformist her mother Esther wishes for. As for me, reading about her, I'm finding it difficult swapping from one century to another and back again; so many characters! And though she's easy to read, their living style seems more formal compared to now. Wonder if anything will develop that'll be worth the focus and locus mantra? Can't say I'm super confident there's a massive mystery anywhere in this but, I have to admit, it's interesting gaining an insight into how things were only half a century ago. Obviously too, I'm not creating these characters; they're not of my imagination and therefore not up to whatever tricks I can imagine and attribute with impunity. They existed, were flesh and blood. Must admit, though, it would be good to find evidence of dirty deeds such as my mum would relish! Fingers would fly over the keyboard then! A better idea of their looks, their appearance, would have been useful too; there were cameras in the early 1900s, even before that – silver plate efforts, daguerreotypes, as James has told me. Surely some likenesses should be around somewhere from that time?

Now, here's a postcard in Katherine's writing, assuring her mother she wouldn't delay her return – perhaps from that visit to Rosalie in Melbourne? No stamp. No date. The card was seemingly never posted. Perhaps a telephone call sufficed – if they used that machine so detested! The wording indicates Esther was missing her daughter and Katherine was reassuring her. There's a short note attached to the postcard in another's untidy handwriting, signed 'Will'. Ahah! Click on recorder.

This must be from William, to Esther, his sister? Untangling all these writings, they're like a spider's web, all sticky and wanting to stay in place. But now I read that William was suggesting Katherine, his niece, go over to England with him; he would pay the fare. He would invite his other niece, Rosalie, too. Oh, wow! Lucky young women! I had to save for years to put my backpack over my shoulder and head overseas. Can't complain; interesting couple of years.

Now Sally, forget Scotland and Inverness; forget Bali and Singapore. Told Granny Kath all about those trips when I came home, photos by the hundred! Cost me another fortune to have them all developed, now it's digital and…ah well. Now c'mon, Sally, focus! Back to the 1930s and 40s. Hmm.

William, Katherine's uncle, writes he was aware Katherine was impatient with having to wait a year before entering college and similarly that 'Ess' worried that Katherine's impulsiveness and restlessness might test her and everyone else as she had already called her year in waiting a wasted time. Uncle William said he knew Katherine was not one to conform. Hmm…I think I'm cottoning on to that now, having read some of her stuff.

I put it down and see a single-page letter signed by Esther and addressed to Erica, William's wife, over in the Riverland. That's Rosalie's home ground. This is dated J/29. Is that January or July 1929? Much earlier than Katherine's stay with Rosalie, anyway. Esther is saying William will take Katherine with him over to England after next Christmas when he plans to take his boys to school. He also wanted to inspect his house there; the one in Kendal left to him by his grandfather, their mother Beatrice's father. It had been rented for a long while and William was deciding what to do with it. Esther seems uncertain. Also another note from Esther to Doc Elena, her own doctor. In Hahndorf. I'm intrigued, but it's torn at the end of the last line…

Elena, I wonder if you could loan me a copy of Mrs Stope's book on planning families. I'm not sure of the title but I'm sure you know of it. Perhaps I might even have a chance to talk to you as to have the book in the house, well I wouldn't want Frank to see it!

I really need to know what I should say to the girls as they grow more independent, certainly to Katherine. I have tried but I think I need more tact, or perhaps to know the proper biological terms to confuse her with my knowledge! She tends to fly off the handle when I suggest talking of intimate matters and Mrs Blum has made me aware of a little flightiness between Katherine and the Schmidt boy and that concerns me, because she says it's not her place to tell stories, but I should perhaps be prepared to talk to Katherine. I feel myself quite uncertain about voicing my own motherly concerns, Elena, as Katherine is quite unaware.

Hmm. I doubt K is unaware of much at all. Perhaps her mother meant aware of her attractiveness? I know of Marie Stopes's family planning theories – no easy contraception back then. It's holding my attention and…here's something, a clutch of papers with a pin in the corners…

Katherine

10

14 December 1930

Dear journal, I'm going to England with Uncle William after Christmas when he takes his boys! Oh, wonderful. And Mum knew all along, was just testing me out. I know she would really like me to stay on here and help her, even forget about teaching, but I know she won't force me. It's a wonderful chance to see the world and I'm so delighted. Kris, so his sister Anna told me, doesn't want me to go, says he'll miss me. He actually told her that Ralph nagged at Mum about my staying in the business, and her chat with me was to please him. He'll always be her favourite. Kris said me staying here had its good points: he and I could meet up whenever he came home from university. I'm still angry at that – how dare he think I'll run to him when convenient!

Of course I shall miss Kris; he's the first boy ever to kiss me – well, nicely enough that I like it – but it was all of last Easter ago. Since then, well, I've been to his place quite often with Anna, his sister. She and I were in the same grade at school for years but only started being friendly last year. She doesn't like playing netball either, so we'd duck out of it as much as we could. She used to breed the sheepdogs in their old foundry on the property or raise late lambs and calves at times, so it was always kept warm in there. Kris and I used to go in there at times to escape from the others in his family – they have eight young boys! Anna doesn't like Rosalie. Rosalie says she's just jealous and wants Ralph to dance at her feet.

Mrs Blum is relieved I'm going away, so she said. I was a bit upset till she explained she saw us that time up behind the showroom and says that is not how a good girl behaves with a young man. Rubbish! It was Mum who told me to learn about myself! Mrs Blum has been our housekeeper for years and she promised not to tell Mum if I bake a stack of gingerbread tomorrow for her. Her hands freeze up too often nowadays, she says, when she mixes things. It's her rheumatics. (Did I spell that all right?) I don't know why she thinks Kris is adventurous – her word. He doesn't have many new ideas. He says we have to act naturally and I agree. He and I have been the very best of friends for months now. Why don't parents watch their sons as closely as they nag us girls?

Ralph is very fussy about behaving properly (he preaches it often enough) but I do know he and Anna cuddle up, because she told me, so if they do it, why can't I? She actually said his kisses give her a thrill! I'm sure Mrs Blum hasn't told Mum about me and Kris, though, or Mum would have said so. I will miss Kris but he does seem to expect me to be with him a lot lately; says he likes how we are together. So he should.

The thought of travelling overseas is wonderful! I can't let Mum think I'm excited, though, or she'll start thinking I'll be sick again like I was at the end of term; exam pressure, she said it was. I think she likes to give us labels; says I'm highly strung. I certainly disliked being nauseous and being dosed with that syrup of figs. But highly strung makes me feel like the sides of ham strung up on the ceiling in the scullery. But to spend weeks on a ship and reach the other side of the world, that *is* so exciting!

I'll be able to see the places the oldies talk about – even dear old Oma has asked me to visit a place called Barwell if possible. It's in England near a river called Tweed. Not at all German! It's where she was born. I'll have to look at some maps. Mum has agreed and so has Dad, reluctantly, but he says he can't understand the appeal of the place – England, that is. When Oma married Opa, there was muttering in his church – feelings were strong because she was not of the faith. And Dad still has a measure of resentment because of his German heritage, says Mum. It's all because of the way his people here in Hahndorf were treated during the war.

Uncle William is paying for Rosalie as well and she is positively ecstatic! He says we're both his nieces and it's quite correct. He waited till Rosalie arrived before telling us. Rosie – and I prefer to call her that – has written to the JC Williamson folk in Melbourne, the Taits I think, asking if they will write her a testimonial to present to their people in London. She said that the company are concerned because audiences are down. We tend to forget there is a depression on or, as Uncle William calls it, an economic downturn. Rosie heard from her Gran'pa Smythe that he went to the movies in Melbourne and the Fox Movietone News has what they call full sound! She's still film crazy – I'm sure that's her aim when she's in London.

I discovered Mum has quite a soft spot for Rosie from when she went over to Cumquats farm to put flowers on Gran'mama's and Gran'papa's graves. That was in 1926 and I was still at school of course, and Rosie went around the farm with her because her dad, my Uncle George, was concerned for her. He calls Mum 'Ess', short for Esther. My brother Ralph cares more for Rosie than he does for me and she's only his cousin. She doesn't mind. She likes men's attention, she says, just as long as they don't act fresh, and Ralph would never take advantage. I'm sure he's too righteous to do anything wrong, but I'm not really sure what she means.

You never can tell with Rosie. She talks in a language I don't understand at times; I think it's the influence of the theatre life. Ralph sees her as one of his projects, I know. He was pleasant enough with me when I told him I like Kris. Kris and Ralph left school a year ago together and they're best mates. Ralph is working in the business here but Kris wants to go to Melbourne University next year. So, though he wants me around, he won't be here either!

But as for me, Uncle William says there are good schools in Kendal and I may be able to study some teaching methods in the schools or something before I come home and enter college. I can return with him or stay on longer, so he says. Mum is ready to agree to my staying on but not Dad – yet.

We're to travel on a liner called the RMS *Otranto* leaving from Outer Harbour at 5 p.m. on Thursday 8 January. So soon! Uncle W. says it's not a scheduled passenger run; it's a mail ship with limited passengers and no one else is booked from Melbourne so it will take only us, as he understands. We embark – I love that word – at Outer Harbour, where it arrives at eight in the morning. It'll take on freight like boxes of Australian butter and crates and sacks of flour. All that from our Australian paddocks – cows and wheat. Also it's carrying some farming equipment made here in Australia that's better than the British (says Uncle). Exciting. It takes on the passengers of course and they include Uncle W, me, Rosalie, Stephen and Nicholas. And Doc Elena's coming too. It'll take five or six weeks, according to Uncle W, but he can't be certain as it doesn't have to be in England to pick up passengers. It's to have a refit, ready for the travelling season.

Alicia isn't coming with us – she'll go home to Cumquats before then. Aunt Erica thinks her precious daughter is too young as yet to travel away from home. Alicia is quite happy about it all. Jacinta moped a bit yesterday but she's too busy with her projects to leave them untended for too long. Goodness knows what she'll do next after that kangaroo kerfuffle. I wondered why Uncle William says how Aunt Erica and Uncle George will look after Cumquats Farm! It's the Symonds family's heritage.

Oh, I'm so excited! Mum says I must go shopping in Adelaide and because Charles Birks has a big sale just after Boxing Day, she and I will shop for a coat, boots and hat. I have to make my dresses and as many of my undergarments as I can, so I'll be opening up the Singer. Dear old Mrs Blum says she'll help me but said I need to lose my puppy fat first! How dare she! Rosalie's Aunt Faith in Melbourne and her Gran'pa Smythe are going to buy her wintry things and put them onto the *Otranto* while it berths in Melbourne before leaving to come to Adelaide. So all is organised. You know, journal, I can see I'll be too busy to write much in your pages for quite a while. Life is all about experience and Oma has bought me a Box Brownie camera as a Christmas present, and some rolls of film. It is incredible that I'll be able to take photographs of places and people and whatever I like! Rosie's brothers Aaron and Alex plan to come to wave us off at Outer Harbour.

I wonder if Kris will come? Or maybe…

Sally

11

Tuesday, 3 April 2018

Bit of a surprise, that. Those names. Action is promised, although –
again – there's a bit torn off! And mention of a camera? But Rosalie's
brothers' names! I didn't know of them. When my twins were born,
Dad did say twins were in the family but to have the same names is
surely more than coincidence! I'd heard of Stephen James and Nicholas
Peter from somewhere and Granny had spoken of her brother Ralph,
who was a priest – no, a pastor – when he died. But James chose our
boys' names, so surely it is just coincidence? Or was he grandstanding
about heritage again? I picked up my mobile.

'Mum, did you know of Alex and Aaron Symonds?'

'Oh. Not much, dear, but your dad did – they were Granny Kath's
cousins and she was very fond of them. She was upset to hear Alexander
died – talked to your dad about them, so he said, when she was upset
about outliving everyone. That Alexander was a politician, for the True
Blue Mob, as Gran called it. From the Renmark family. Alex went
over the border to the Victoria parliament – was always close to his
mother's family, the Smythes. His twin Aaron died in the vineyard, he
was quite a famous vigneron, you know. His sons run it now. It was
some accident with machinery. Look, I was on my way out of the door
to come round when you rang. Found something else for you…you'll
like these. Quite something. See you soon.'

'Oh noooo! Mum, I…'

She'd clicked off.

She turns up about an hour later carrying a strange half-metre-
square bundle, pretty solid, sides about twenty-five centimetres deep.
Firmly studded top and bottom, it seems, but there's a zipper.

'Mum! That's one of Granny's lumpy wicker chair cushions from her sunroom!'

'So I now realise, Missy. And your toast is smoking!'

I spring up. Oh, not again! I need to focus my mind.

She follows me in to my kitchen, dumping her burden on the kitchen floor. I recognise it. I've sat on it many times over the years. I can only stare.

'Heaven's sake, Sally, look here. The zipper's broken and the studs don't go right through. Just feel it.'

A tentative poke, then I pick it up. It crackles.

I look at Mum. 'More papers. Stashed, hidden, secreted – too carefully stuffed away. These were meant for burning with the old chairs, not meant for anyone's eyes. Right?'

She was wide-eyed. 'My thoughts exactly. I didn't know they were there, and I really thought it was old rubbish, nearly threw it all out. Very sneakily hidden. Had a quick look. Could be what you've been waiting for.' She giggled. 'And me!'

'Mum, I hope so. So far, the stuff in the old case is reasonably interesting but doesn't catch the imagination. Family stuff mostly, with no real, regular journal items with sequels, consequences. If we're chasing mysteries, Mum, as you're convinced, we need organisation.'

She winks. Which reminds me.

'Mum, before Granny Kath went to England – and she was only seventeen – she had a serious boyfriend who didn't want her to go. He was called Kris with a K. She certainly wasn't just the quiet writer-academic-type I'd thought! Had you heard of him?'

That brought a wide grin of glee. 'Ahah – is this the germ of a story after all? I remember you asking me once before, ages ago, what it was that Granny Kath wouldn't say but seemed in some ways eager for you to know.' She turns to go then swivels on her toes. 'No lies no pack drill, Sally. I think she probably wanted you to learn of her doings in this way on paper and not face to face. This way spares her blushes.'

'Well, seems odd. The way this stuff is packed, it's unlikely she wanted it found, don't you agree? Might throw some light on the mystery you long for!'

She gave me a hasty 'mwah' on the cheek and was off again muttering something about 'Light's going and I need to keep my eye on the painter.'

I have to smile. That poor chap's no doubt enjoying her absence so she can't be peering over his shoulder. And surely the weather's too warm for paint? Well, I know she had to wait for weeks over the Christmas/New Year period. He went away somewhere with the excuse it wasn't good to paint in the hot weather anyway. Mum wasn't too pleased at the delay; she's no easy taskmistress, nor has she mellowed with age. She's well into her seventies and – given a chance – she'd be up the ladders doing it herself. Thankfully, not! As for blushes? Well now, there's a thing; was Granny all ablush? That's an intriguing thought.

Granny Kath seems to be on the move in her memoirs, physically and emotionally. I really should be more domestically inclined; even my mother is busy redecorating. I sip a glass of water and gaze outside into my neglected rear garden. It demands some TLC; even the petunias look limp and they usually withstand the worst the summer can throw at them. A flutter of tiny honeyeaters are flapping and fighting for the best blooms in the eremophila bush and the bird bath is low on water. This is 2018 and here in South Australia – all down to global warming, apparently – we're enduring one of our hottest and driest ever summers, and even now as we move towards autumn. I move away from the window; the garden will have to wait.

My mind has been chronologically zigzagging hither and thither – in England, Poland, all Europe and early Australia – as I try to transform paper memories from Granny Kath into actual people having to endure actual situations.

Two days later. That last torn page with the boys' names – frustrating. She's still liking that Kris, wondering if he'll come to farewell them onto their ship.

Oh, Granny Kath! What a tangled web we weave when first we

practise to deceive. Who said that? Hmm…*Katherine's Web*. A title? Yay! I like it.

'So, Granny. This Avril: is she a doll or could she be something else? The cause of your puppy fat perhaps? I'm suspicious. What did you do with her during the years between your leaving to go overseas and coming back – with Sam, who married my mum and who I know as Dad. What did you *do* for all that time?

And now this solidly secreted bumff, as Dad would call it. Intriguing.

Next day. I'm having a break from the past, hitting the present. It's another barbecue for the boys tonight; this time to celebrate Alex buying a house. I promised a pavlova. The boys brought a few of their mates and girlfriends back with them and it wasn't long before Alex had the barbie going and Aaron was fishing for beers. Luckily, the weather's on their side.

Can't banish Granny Kath altogether from the day. Even as I busy myself grating celeriac and fennel, I'm dwelling on that first page of Katherine's memoirs. Mum said recently that it must be an edifying experience matching the young Katherine with the Granny Kath I had known best. I sense also that she has a prurient interest in this voyage to England on which the girls are to embark. So, salad complete, I did the 'hello everybody' thing then retreated back indoors with a lovely glass of shiraz poured by Aaron.

I'm determined to resist fossicking too widely in that new load of papers until I've determined some date structure – or some other organisation. Sipping my vino, nibbling on almonds, my place is my low thinking chair; and my concern, Granny Kathleen's secrets.

12

A few days later. Last time I wrote, a kerfuffle outdoors broke into my wine-induced reminiscences about Granny's little tea ceremony. Didn't manage too much thinking! Great excitement: James had turned up – in a taxi, no less! Opportunely, the barbie, and the boys' mates, were going full blast. I relaxed. So good for the boys to share some time with their father. It turned into quite a party. James no longer has to wage peace, as they call it, in the Middle East but his regiment has been deployed in Darwin for more than three months; much safer but still some distance away.

Thankfully we now have Skype and some other communication tools I use occasionally, but the boys are always on some device or another and their mobiles are miniature computers. Unless he's sent off to some obscure posting in the islands, we can keep in touch. He only has a few more years to serve – well, he plans to retire on 7 July 2022, his sixtieth birthday. Then it's home to build his business. Robotronic or mechatronic applications is his thing; his is an organised and logical mind, as I'm reminded! The boys both studied the subject and its various physical and scientific applications at university; different courses but both have started promising careers using their physics abilities. Hopefully they'll support their father in his plans but we'll have to wait and see.

Alex has just bought this house and I know his father will want to look it over, as do I. The boy's trying to gain a foothold in a narrowing market which Aaron, more the financial one, explains will happen. I still refer to them as 'boys', which is a bit ridiculous, because they're coming up for their twenty-fourth birthdays. I'm trying to persuade Aaron to do something similar – not that I don't enjoy their company but it's time they settled down or at least moved out of their parents' home, as my mother reminds me! Alex's had this same girlfriend now for a couple of years, pleasant lass, and we like each other enough, so maybe it won't be long before…well, before!

It's so good to have James around the place again; we can talk as parents talk. Also, it's been a relief for me, moving ahead from the middle of last century to the here and now; to the present and the future and how we fit into it all. We've been discussing our boys, as parents will. James agrees the boys should be striking out on their own by now. He thinks they're just too comfortable living at home with me, as he puts it, dancing attendance upon them. I protest at that – there is also the cost of buying a house.

They're both intelligent young men anyway; they may be twins but they're different in many physical respects. Alex has hair the colour of a crow's plumage and as glossy; Aaron has red hair, quite a lovely colour actually, but he hates it. His friends say that his beard, when he tried to grow one, made him look like Prince Harry! Granny Kath once said to him – he was in his early teens and touchy about it – that he takes after her sister Jacinta, that she had glorious hair too. Oh goodness, I'm starting to think like Granny Kath; it's this heritage thing again.

James moves over to the cupboard. 'I fancy a leisurely whisky, Sal. You? Or a cup of tea?'

Tea appeals and in due course he brings one over to me as I waken from my thoughts.

He sits down, his eyes on my notes. 'Goodness knows what those boys have been up to in the kitchen – cups and glasses out all over the surfaces.' He leans back in his chair. 'Y'know, I learned of Jacinta when our twins were born and we saw Aaron's red hair. I wonder if he did inherit it from her? Anyway, your dad mentioned her dying and how he was in grade two at school – funny how kids relate events to school's years – and Granny Kath was really upset when she received the letter. He'd never known this Aunt Jacinta, so that day he just gave his mum a kiss and went off into school as normal.'

'I can't remember any mention of Jacinta from Gran. I think there's so much yet to find among these papers from the cushion. You know,

James, I'm sure they weren't meant to be found. The suitcase: do you reckon that could have been a decoy? To keep us from the real stuff?'

He laughed. 'You're as bad as your mum, wanting to dig the dirt… Just think. This Great-Aunt Jacinta died in 1947, your dad said, when all of Europe was hit by a fierce winter – all of Europe wore a blanket of ice. She fell through the ice and couldn't climb out again. Actually, that was probably after the turn of the year – call it 1948. Not a pleasant way to go. She was trying to save a fawn, a baby deer of some breed anyway, that had fallen through a fishing hole.'

'Yes, I read of her being some kind of animal rights activist but I didn't know much else.'

'Your dad once mentioned Jacinta falling pregnant but asked me never to mention it to your Gran. Looking back, I think I can understand her reluctance to talk about Jacinta at the time, and perhaps her pain. It seems your father ruled the family with his religion – okay, nothing wrong with religion – but his seemed particularly damning of anything straying from the chosen path. Jacinta was only in her thirties when she drowned and Dad told me she had two little girls – twins of course, what else – but no one knew who the father was. Your dad also cautioned me against mentioning them to Gran because he knew, from her, of the strain that prevailed when it was known she was pregnant, and why remind her…'

'Only now, knowing Katherine's persistent liaison with that Kris, do I suspect she had become pregnant and this Avril to be real, not a doll, and therefore it's all significant, this turmoil in the family.'

'Sal, you said your mum seemed genuinely unaware of any Avril when you first saw that photo in the old suitcase. Your dad told me his grandmother Esther – wife of Francis, or Frank if you'd rather – collapsed mentally because of the strain of trying to maintain a level of normality between her husband and their youngest daughter and that led to her death. I wonder if she was one of those hysterical types? Somehow, I think not. Granny Kath always called them strong women, didn't she. However, constantly fretting over a husband's attitude to one of your children, walking on eggshells, as they say, for months even years on end, would wear you out.'

He pulled at the cushion's zipper. 'I've trawled through some of this stuff and you really must look at it. Some is journal stuff. And this – how apt – is a note, bit blotchy but mentioning this very business. I don't know the handwriting. Here…have a looksee. Oh, I think it's Esther's writing, Granny Kath's mother. It says, I think, "Your Papa is calling Jacinta wild and a stain on her family." Oh, dearie me. This next bit, under the ink blotches, seems to indicate he thinks it is Esther's fault. He says "because you are not of the church", implying her morals were somehow lacking. Bit rough, huh, blaming her mother. I read earlier that Katherine's brother Ralph is also a stickler for propriety, talking of cutting off one's nose to spite the face. Jacinta's twin, Arthur, kept her children in Adelaide and he and his wife later adopted them after looking after them for Jacinta while she went abroad. When were her children born? Early '40s perhaps? Did she leave home to live with her twin and his wife – the ones she later left her daughters with while she travelled? I hope I can find out why she left this country at such a time. And how – because the world was again at war. She certainly was quite a colourful character from early on, if that school memo Katherine had written about the culling of kangaroos is an indication! So many questions yet to find the answers to, Sal. Keep digging?

'You know, James, I've just thought – her children must be in their seventies by now, heading for eighty, nearly Mum's age, and I've no idea where they might have ended up. I wonder whether they were boys or girls or same gender. Worries me a bit that they could be living just down the road and we wouldn't know if they had married names. Perhaps it's not so strange that Granny Kath never mentioned them – well, not to me. Illegitimacy then was really looked down upon, considered a sin against the church and a stigma, a stain on the whole family and she, Gran, I'm certain, had a lot of nastiness aimed at her. I really should be focusing on Katherine anyway, as exclusively as this family network, this web of names and nationalities, will allow. More and more I want to know about this Avril – wax doll she is not, the more I think about it. She's at the bottom of all this, betcha!'

He yawned. 'Come on, Sal – let's get off to bed. It's late and I'm flying back tomorrow afternoon. Need to pack in the morning.'

Next afternoon. James had tried to extend his leave to cover Easter – with the boys going away for the period, we two could have had some quiet time together. It was not to be. That's the military life.

But while here, he admitted his interest towards Katherine's 'letters bounty' as he calls it. He suggested using the computer to help plot and sequence her travels from her departure to England in 1931 to her return. He it was who picked out from the suitcase selection an envelope addressed to my grandad with his service number and name but the address blacked out. In it is the photo of young Granny holding baby Samuel Francis, and it was James who made the link that it was the one David never saw. Surely there must be others, the ones she took herself, among all this documentation? Because James understands the Service life, he feels deeply for the young airman who was Granny Kath's husband and the awful dangers he had to face back then. What he calls all this generation jumping has intrigued him as much as it has frustrated me.

He has such a logistical approach. With the little time the boys left him unoccupied, he sifted and sorted some of the cushion documents with his orderly precision.

'Haven't time to dig out some more stuff, Sal, too tightly packed to the back edge. But I've set up a table on your computer that's so much quicker at calculating times, dates, ages. Should streamline the sequencing. Should be a lot easier for you to document. You know, some of what I did see is dated and…well, if they're proper journal entries, detailed and factual stuff, quite intriguing! I have an instinct in such things, luv, and I somehow think that the suitcase was just a decoy to keep us happy, that this stuff packed in the unlikely cushion cover was destined – in her mind – to go in the incinerator with the old chairs.'

So he's wanting the stuff documented? What about simply having a looksee and a read?

Now he's returned to Darwin, I've made a decision. Don't know why I didn't think of it earlier. I can possibly find out something about Jacinta's twins via the much vaunted social media. I joined Facebook about a year ago – well, in fact the twins were teasing me about facing up to technology and it was Aaron who joined me up. It has been interesting when occasionally friends I made backpacking overseas contacted me, despite years having flown. All it took was a photo of me taken about twenty years ago – thank you, Alexander.

I haven't looked for ages but I'll ask if any twin girls had a mother Jacinta and were brought up in Adelaide by a Mr and Mrs Arthur Flack. They'll be old ladies by now, no joke. Assuming they were born around 1944/45, they'll be about Mum's age. They'll be grandmothers! However, someone out there might make a connection. I hesitated before posting. James would scoff at me but I'll tell him if I have a result. Not sure where these things go. I'll check in a couple of days if I remember. Now, where was I on these note of Katherine's?

I really must work on a sensible structure for all of her notes and journals – if there are many worthwhile. James was as intrigued as I am about Katherine's writing. The tables he's set up will be a help because focusing sequentially is difficult when they seem to be randomly shoved in deep; they jump from place to place and time to time, person to person. I find there are so many characters popping up all over the place, too many for a reader's focus too – but that's a writer's viewpoint. It's up to me to decide.

So well secured, zippered up! Perhaps I've been slow on the uptake but I am curious about why these things are so well hidden. Maybe like movie censorship they're all M15+. Yay! That would please Mum. I know I'm slow on the uptake but must admit ears are tweaking, palm of hand itching…are they signs? Drama? Secrets? Mum's stubbornly held premise – hidden years? I may have been slow on the uptake but now my curiosity has been tweaked and there are questions emerging, and I want some answers. The one entry on my knee, dated and its pages' edges turned over to be held together: seems they've arrived in England. Okay, pressing on!

Katherine

13

23 February 1931

Dear journal, we have finally arrived in Uncle William's Kendal house. It's quite a pleasant countryside. Everything is so green, the trees and the grass and the fields. There's melted snow lying around the grassy edges, though. On the train they were talking about a thaw and were pleased because it should now grow warmer and the days longer. We actually berthed in Tilbury Docks – near London – a week ago but there was some sort of riot from a Seaman's Union – or that's what I understood. Then we had to wait for all the freight to be landed before we could! We had a night in a hotel and caught the train to Kendal.

I miss Kris and so wish I could tell him what's happening to me, to us. He'll be in Melbourne by now enjoying his university life. Seems to me that men get away with anything and everything. He it was who said he knew what to do and what not to do and he made the most noise enjoying it. I've decided I don't love him any more but I just wish I could let him know!

One of the big shocks we found out on the last few days on the ship was that Anna Pavlova, that lovely ballet dancer, died in Holland about a month ago. One of the crew told Rosalie when she was doing some barre exercises on the railings. He only mentioned it when she talked of ballet. Why didn't we know this from the telegraph thing system? And I think we were in that African port about then but I didn't write a lot on the ship because I was sick so often. Rosalie asked one of the ship's officers and he said he would check for her and said yes, she died on the 23rd of last month – just a month ago! She was cremated and buried at Golders Green in London, so he said.

Rosalie has been incredibly upset since we landed and is still subdued when she thinks about it happening. We few passengers weren't told because the captain didn't think it of interest. He was keeping Uncle informed about the financial matters arising from this Depression. England is affected more than South Australia, according to Uncle when I asked him for more information. Not that he tells me much at all. In fact, he's growing annoyed when I don't eat at each meal, says he doesn't want a sick girl on his hands and I have to pick myself up – it's only a matter of training my sea legs.

I do wish that's all it was. I confessed to Doc Elena I was worried I might be expecting. She seemed less surprised that I expected and then admitted Mum had asked her advice after Mrs Blum dobbed me and Kris in…sneak! She'd been watching me and had begun to see signs.

'Doc Elena, Mum told me to grow up and find out about things, so I did. I was angry with her at the time. Kris was becoming a bit insistent and Mum was all Ralph this and Ralph that as if I did nothing around the place to help in the business. Guess I just wanted to show her I was grown-up and sensible too. Silly of me, I know. If I'd known this trip was to be offered, well…'

'Katherine, you were naughty, irresponsible, to do this because you know how it happens, so do not pretend to me you are innocent. It was certainly not grown-up behaviour. However, I do feel for you because you have yet to inform your parents and also your uncle, who has paid for your travel – to help you in a career, so he explained to me. That is up to you. I will say nothing, to allow you to think things through. I'll keep shtum.'

I'm scared to tell anyone else. But I daren't tell Uncle the reason I'm not well. Doc Elena tells me I'll get over it, that some women do have sickness till quite late in the development and that if I drink lemonade – and there's an endless supply of that – it'll make me feel better. And she's planning to take a trip to Poland, and if I haven't told Uncle by then, she will do so.

I promised Mum I would write as soon as possible, so I wrote from that African port. I didn't go ashore anywhere, though. I've been so very sick. I grew sick and tired of the blue, blue sea too. Rosalie thinks it's hilarious that I spent so much time in my bunk on the ship; she loves to tease and laughs at my lack of sea legs, as she puts it. She thinks that's quite a joke since she first heard Uncle telling me off.

Uncle W told her off a couple of times for flirting (that's what he called it) with the sailors and officers on board. I didn't blame her. One of them, an engineer officer, is an absolute stunner, looks like a film star. I nearly burst out about my baby a couple of times but thinking of Elena, and Uncle William's possible reaction, held me back. If Rosie's told off for flirting by Uncle W, I dread his reaction when he finally knows about me.

Soon, Doc Elena says, we have to tell him, but not until she makes her travel plans to Czechoslovakia – I thought it was Poland – so she knows when she'll leave and come back. She has promised to be with me when I need her. She wants to go within a few days because we're later arriving here than she planned. Turns out, journal, she *is* Polish! She says she has some cousins in Prague and they would welcome her for a stay because it's happier for Poles in that country now than it used to be and she believes also the Germans may attack Czechoslovakia in a few years. She might be away three or four weeks, no longer, but she says I'll be all right, the baby won't come till at least the middle of April, and I must just remember to wear loose tops and my pleated skirt and not eat too much bread and cake.

Uncle William says Kendal is called the Old Grey Town. Well, it is – grey, that is: rows of grey stone houses and endless grey stone walls. The sky is grey today also. Rosalie wants to go for a walk to look around and I don't want to; it's drizzling rain and all that dirty grey old snow I can see from the window is melting away. I found a decent book to read here on a shelf so Steve and Nick have walked with her down the Beastbanks hill to see what shops are open. Aunt Erica gave Uncle William a list of stuff to buy on our arrival so the others will bring something back for a couple of days' supplies. Uncle William and Doc Elena have gone out into the garden to check if any veg are growing.

Aunt Erica planted a rowan tree when they were here some years ago and Doc Elena asked to see it. She dislikes concealing my condition from him when he has been so generous and I suspect she'll tell him about me and I'm really scared how Uncle W will take the news…

Later. Oh, my goodness. I expected trouble and I have it. I don't know if Uncle W is more angry with me or Elena.

He came into my room when I was reading and burst out, 'How can you be so wanton! So deceitful and so brazen to keep it a secret from me! And when I offered to bring you to increase your aptitude for a teaching career!' Then he went all quietly angry and said, 'Kindly refrain from telling Rosalie your dreadful secret. She is off to London soon. Nor will you tell my boys, who will be driving up to the school on Wednesday for an initial interview. Your behaviour is not to colour their opportunities, do you hear me?' His grey eyes were as dark and cold as all the grey slates and stones in this town.

I think that for the first time I am feeling really, awfully ashamed. He stormed out of the room and Doc Elena slipped in almost straight away. She gave me a hug.

'I'm in his bad books too, my girl. I'm just glad we were outside in the garden when he tore into me. It's not only anger with him. He believes I cheated him and should have known better…all that kind of thing he spat out at me. I am now so glad I insisted on paying my own fare. Now he'll tell your mum and I have to face her recriminations too…'

That thought chills my bones, journal. Oooooh. I hate myself!

Sally

14

Saturday, 21 April 2018

We had visitors from up north and did the touristy thing over the last two weeks. They were sorry to miss James and the boys. They'll catch up with the boys later next week as they return for an overnight stay before catching the aircraft to Singapore.

So, busy as I was, I only did a speed read of Katherine's notes. My instincts were right. She was expecting. Odds are it'll be that Avril photo – but I'll be patient and wait till I dig up some more. Poor girl; so different then from now; and now, well, our mothers tell us what's what before it happens, don't they? None of the silly modesties of years ago – I'm reminded of her mother asking the doc for a copy of Mrs Stopes's book – acted too late. And we even have the pill now!

However, I remembered I'd posted on Facebook about the Flach (or Flack) twin girls. I hadn't mentioned how Jacinta died but a Melanie commented on my site that her grandmother's mother was Jacinta and she died in France rescuing a fawn from an icy pond! Has to be! Her grandmother was Irene Simms née Flack and is alive but in a nursing home with Alzheimers. Oh dear. The grandmother's twin was Suzanne and died from breast cancer about ten years ago after living in France all her life. Oh dear again; how sad. This Melanie did say she is encouraging her mother to send me a message. I hope she does. I'm so glad to know of those children, though. I'll tell Mum I know of them, later, when I hear from this Melanie's mother. If I do.

My boys have yet another few days in the Grampians – all that climbing and hiking, they'll enjoy it. Well, I know they are – Aaron sent me a photo, of Alexander leaning over a crevasse high up on a peak called the Pinnacle! Eek!

No cooking, so I can devote some time to this… Now it's back to another group of entries James placed in order for me. I want to know. Katherine's writing is fluent and so easy to read, more a novel than a diary entry. I shall let her tell her own story as much as I can, but I'll use my recorder when relevant…

Katherine

15

Wednesday, 25 February 1931

Uncle W has driven off up to Windermere to the school. He is to leave the boys there for the day, to be assessed, he said. Sounds horrific.

Rosie and I decided to walk into Kendal town and have a look round. It's quite a historical place. There's a castle here on a hill that was owned by the Parr family and Catherine Parr was the last wife of old King Henry VIII – the one who survived him. It's quite a walk but we'll see it sometime, if not today. We found a shop that makes meat pies and the smell was gorgeous! I persuaded Rosie to buy one and we did and went into a park up a nearby Maude Street to find a seat. It was *delicious*! Then Rosie spoiled it all; she said I shouldn't have eaten it.

'Just look at your stomach, Kath! You are positively rotund! It's all that sitting down on the boat. I, of course, did my barre exercises at the rail each day. Kept me slim. Kath, you are *enormous*.'

I swear she spoke in capital letters. I nearly let her in on the secret in protest. Thankfully, I did not!

We met Doc Elena on the walk back up the hill. I was puffing and panting. Rosalie kept chattering on about me getting so fat. I could have strangled her! Doc sent me a question with her eyebrows and I shook my head. She nodded, satisfied. She and Rosie started discussing the best train into London. Rosalie needs to wait for a letter back from the JC Williamson contacts before she leaves here, but Elena wants to leave on next Tuesday 3 March. That's the best day for her connections, wherever they're going to and from. I want Rosie to go before I can't lace myself in any longer. I would *die*, positively *die*, if she found out.

The two boys are now in a frenzy of uniforms and kit stuff. The Easter term has started and the boys will be a week late apparently but they don't care. Easter Sunday is on 5 April and that's when they'll come home next, or actually on the Thursday before, so it'll be a short time away, which Uncle W likes the sound of. The boys are hoping to drive up on Friday so they can settle into their dorms over the weekend. Consequence? Uncle W asked me to please sew all their name tapes on their clothing *tout de suite*, even their socks for goodness sakes! He's *just out for revenge* (but he did say please).

The boys have enrolled for a rowing and water safety elective and Steve borrowed my copy of *Swallows and Amazons* for hints. I warned them not to damage it, and they must read it before they go. It's the one I bought down the street and it's only recently been published. I imagine that any school on the shore of Lake Windermere would be water crazy! They are nice enough boys, though, so I don't really mind and when Rosie's gone too, well, I'll have time on my hands.

She just came running into my room. 'Letters here are pushed through your front door, Kath. How cute – and one's for me! I'm to meet with some producing team on Friday – what a rush! All because we're late arriving. There's a show called the *White Horse Inn* at the Coliseum starting in April. That's in London. I have the address to go to in their letter here. Oh Katherine, if I'm good enough, I might get a part! They want dancers and my JC recommendation seems to be a good one! Oh, I might be in, *in*! I'll have to start from the back line, though, in what they call the rear chorus, but who cares! I'm to go for a proper audition next Monday if they like me when we meet Friday. They'll book me a place in a women's hostel called the YHA or something, starting from Wednesday night. That's only tomorrow! Will you help me pack? And isn't life wonderful!'

Of course it is; couldn't be better! At least she'll be gone before I can no longer hide my bump.

Tuesday, 3 March

Hello journal. Doc Elena went this morning on the train. It was all a bit of a hurry for her but we had landed later than we thought, she said. She'll be away three or four weeks, no longer, but she said again I'll be all right; to the best of her instincts, the baby won't come till at least the middle of April. She urged me yet again to wear loose tops and my pleated skirt and not eat too much bread and cake. Truthfully, I think she wanted to move out of the pervading angry atmosphere. Uncle W drove her down in his new car, hired from a garage on Sandes Avenue, and it seemed later they had struck a truce. I wish I could do the same.

My Symonds cousins Steve and Nick apparently survived their interview. They talked of little else at tea that night. Uncle W had a letter last Friday confirming their enrolments. I wondered what he would have done with all that uniform stuff if they had been turned down! I helped the new housekeeper, showing her where things were kept. She's not living in. She was recommended by the lady next door, a Mrs Graham, who Uncle W and Erica met when they were here before. So Mrs Smiles (yes, really) will come in at 6 o'clock each morning and leave at 6 o'clock at night. Uncle W says the washing of the dinner dishes will be up to whoever has enjoyed the dinner each evening.

Well, Rosie's still here tonight but I'm willing to wager she'll disappear upstairs to pack or something when the table's dirty dishes are cleared. Not one for the basics, as my dad would say. After all, she is to be famous, huh. Sorry, journal, but I'm growing tired of all Rosie's plans and I'm stuck here, shortly to commit myself to a baby's routine – for life. All right! I know it's my own fault.

Wednesday, 4 March

Didn't manage much journal writing today. By the weekend, as Uncle W calls Saturdays and Sundays, I must have all the name tags sewn onto the boys' school clothes. This morning the boys went out with him to look around for books, pens or things like that. Rosie went in the car with them because Uncle W is dropping her off at the railway on his way – says he needs to know she safely catches the train. Phew, what a hurried packing up she made! I helped her but she really doesn't have much to take with her. So now they're all gone and it's just me and Mrs Smiles for a whole day. Bliss!

Later in the afternoon, I loosened my skirt to sit and sew and Mrs S came in with a cup of tea and saw my bump.

She stopped and looked at me, then her lips wobbled a bit and she started to cry. 'Oh, yer poor lasssie!' She patted my knee a couple of times then said, 'Yer secret's safe wi'me. Never worry,' and went off before I had time to say anything at all. Perhaps just as well.

My eyes are actually starting to itch; they're dry with straining to sew. Mrs Smiles pops in with mugs of milky cocoa though at every opportunity. I believe she thinks it's good for me but it's too fattening, I think. She loads it with sugar – and sugar's not cheap to buy either! I'll have to have a word.

Tuesday, 10 March

Uncle William called me to the front room after breakfast. I'd managed all the sewing and packing for boys over the last few days. He'd already told me about the school and the boys' welcome as they checked in their house. Nick is in Coniston house and Steve in Grasmere house. It seems that they'll sleep in different dormitories and I dared to suggest they might find that a bit hard, being so close as twins usually are. Uncle said it would do them good; that competition, mainly in sport, will toughen a boy up a bit. I hope he's right but can't help wondering if Aunt E will agree.

He wanted to tell me that he'd received a telegram from Aunt E in Renmark. Apparently Uncle George is to remarry, and soon. Hmm… He read that Uncle George assures Aunt E it'll be only a quiet affair because his lady friend is a widow with three sons and an elder daughter. Quite a long telegram because Aunt E writes that they're quite a pleasant bunch and will be a great help on the property. So Uncle W said he now has to make decisions of his own: for instance, should they now move to his Adelaide house permanently? I quietly wondered how Rosie will feel at the news. Uncle W said Aunt E. had also telegraphed Rosie.

He seems to have forgiven me a little, actually sharing some of his worries with me about Aunt E: for instance, will she want to stay in Renmark where she has the medical practice or perhaps be willing to move with him into the Adelaide house? I was so glad he seems to have accepted my own situation, if not approving of it. Sorry, journal, if I seem selfish, but I have worries of my own. And I've never been part of the Cumquats bunch, as Mum calls them, so it's hard to feel involved – except for Rosie.

Uncle W did tell me he favours not selling this Kendal house after all – well, not in the foreseeable future; that an increasingly palatable option would be to rent it out or use it as a base for his boys while they're schooling here. As things turn out, he's being quite decent. He sat by the window a while, sipping a whisky and deep in thought, so I picked up my knitting. Then he stood up, looking decisive,' and said to me that if when the baby arrives I wish to stay here with it, that would be permissible. He would continue to employ Mrs Smiles to help me and also to ensure the house was properly maintained for the boys' holidays. He did say I would need to seek a respectable occupation to support myself and the child as soon as practical but I would be welcome, as would Rosie, to stay here whenever the need arises.

That is such a worry off my shoulders! I burst into tears as I thanked him; I am so genuinely touched by his thoughtfulness. What he didn't say was how long he would be staying over here now. Tomorrow he's going down to London on business and says he'll be gone for about a week but will be back in good time for when the boys break up for their Easter short half-term break. That will be from Palm Sunday on 29 March and Easter from the Friday after, 3 April. If the boys have another week after that, oh goodness, journal, it could be cutting it a bit close. I so hope Elena will be back!

Sally

16

My year moves on! All the contents of the case require my undivided attention, as James urged. He hates unresolved curiosity. Me, I enjoy the process of finding the answers. I miss James and his logicality. He has asked that I write my accounts of discovery so that I can email some to him or he can read when he next comes home. What with my screeds adding to Katherine's, I trotted off to Officeworks for some plastic sleeves and buttoned covers. Though I do my notes on the keyboard, they still need printing out and the paper work's piling up!

Quiet few days beckoning. Our boys are now with some Melbourne friends before returning home. They are so lucky to be granted the leave from work the army disallows their dad! And Mum's busy with some CWA open market or something, so hopefully I might make some headway with my research. I've heard nothing more yet from that Melanie on Facebook.

One thing I have done is to verify some dates with my mother – after all, she knows just when missing years occurred! Mum thinks Dad was about eight years old when Gran brought him home to Australia, that's what he told her; that he was in grade two when his mum had the telegram about Jacinta. His father, David, had been killed in 1942. Mum questions the years between 1934 when they married and 1941 when Dad was born. She is so obsessed by gaps, what she calls those missing years. I know where Dad went to school, that he studied accountancy and in time built a successful business but that's all, really. He used to joke that his was an uneventful life; he called it pale in comparison with my mother's. Maybe so, but he was a good, caring Dad to me and I lacked for very little. He liked James from the day they met, and gave us a lovely wedding. Granny Kath loved being the diva that day – he laughed. He loved my boys too, and also the fact that they were yet another pair of twins. I'm still wondering if it was only coincidence that James and I gave our pair those names? I should have asked him when he was here. My dad died in April 2012, on April Fool's Day. Mum called it ironical. I know the date, failed to appreciate her irony.

Katherine Beatrice is the one pulling all the strands together of this wide-ranging band of Australian cousins, aunts, uncles and grandparents, she is the linchpin between the generations. Yet with Granny Kath's dear tired face still flashing into my head, why do I feel that I'm intruding into her life too much? Why were so many of her notes and diary entries kept hidden? She would have known that the little suitcase, so casually placed in Dad's cupboard, would be scanned The buttoned cushion is a very different matter – buttoned and zipped, placed with shabby old wicker chairs; she would have assumed my mum and dad would destroy those without question. The suitcase was, I am sure, a gentle dupe. I reached into the cushion lot.

Ahah, Katherine's moved on a couple of weeks…

Katherine

17

Monday, 23 March 1931

I seem to have managed quite a bit of baby sewing with Uncle away and even my knitting has improved. Mrs Smiles, as it turns out, is quite a dear, keeps me well supplied with hot milky chocolate – an instruction from Uncle W, it seems. Generous thought. Mrs S brings the bottles of milk in with her each morning; she meets the dairy cart in the street and it's lovely creamy milk, seems much more so than at home. She says it's because the cows have such rich pasture. And I'm still marvelling how lush and green all the pastures are, now the snows and the frosts are well behind us.

I'm inclined not to sit and sew today. I feel like going for a walk but Mrs S was shocked at my suggestion – apparently it's not ladylike to parade in the streets being so obviously pregnant, and without an escort. However, I feel quite uncommonly like exercise of a sort so I've brushed and mopped my bedroom floor and after lunch I think I'll perhaps tidy up some of the books in the library. Uncle W has grumbled so often at the untidy state of the shelves in there and I should be able to sort the books alphabetically at least.

Later: it's now three o'clock and I'm a bit concerned because I have a dreadful backache developing. Too much sitting over recent weeks, I think. I do wonder if it's an early warning about the baby but it's not expected yet, Doc Elena thought mid-April. However, when I asked Mrs S if I could have a hot water bottle and she asked why and I told her, she practically turned purple in excitement! Of all things, she has called the local doctor and says she'll stay until he's been to see me. I'm not a little annoyed at her interference. I was told to expect pains, sharp ones, in sequence, whereas this is just a persistent ache.

Well, the doctor came, name of Gerald Soames. Mrs S had been given his name by Uncle W and it appears this Doctor Soames knows of my condition from Uncle W already and has been asked to keep an eye. I'm quite abashed by Uncle's caring; he had been so furiously angry to me when told the news.

Dr Soames performed a most embarrassing examination of me; I was covered in blushes! Mrs S stayed in the room with me all the time, murmuring what was meant to be comfort, I think, but the pain certainly increased as he pressed and pummelled. He left with the words that he may not be needed for at least another twenty-four hours but he was to be called on the telephone at any time; he left a number with Mrs S, who'll stay overnight. Honestly, what a fuss! However, it does seem this baby is nearer to arriving than I thought.

Tuesday evening, 24 March

I don't know what time it happened but I woke after midnight in pain, and I'd wet the bed – or rather the dreadful rubber sheet Mrs S had thought advisable – and then I started to learn what pain is, really is.

Doctor Soames turned up – I think it was in the afternoon. Now it's well into Wednesday the 25th. He smelled of onions and he brought a very starchy nurse with him who performed the most incredibly embarrassing and immodest examination. I just wanted it all to end, the mess, the pain, the smell. I felt the baby arrive and slip out onto another rubber sheet and the nurse grabbed it and took it away to the table while Mrs S mopped around with fluffy towels and hot water. I just wanted it to finish. I asked her if it was a little girl or a boy and she smiled and said it was a girl, with black hair.

I waited for the cry Doc Elena had told me to expect but there was none and I sat up to look over at the nurse who was smacking my baby's feet and then she turned her over and banged her back then onto her front then upside down blowing into her mouth. Then I knew something was horribly wrong but didn't know what to say or do, but Mrs Smiles wouldn't let me move off the bed. Then the doctor nodded at her and she shot off to the telephone again. There was no baby cry, no movement of the little legs I could see on the table. Mrs S came round to me and hugged my shoulders, but she didn't say what I sensed, what I was sure was right, that the baby was dead, that she had died.

Then the door burst open and the Reverend Paulus came into the room – he'd called on Uncle a couple of times. He nodded at me, kissed his stole and moved over to the doctor and they huddled and the doc took out his stethoscope and they huddled again.

Then the Rev turned to me and said, 'Do you have a name?'

I had only thought of one when I expected the babe to arrive in April and if it was a girl. 'Avril.' I said and he baptised the little baby over on the table. Then I burst into awful tears. 'Let me see her! Let me hold her!'

The starchy nurse stiffened in protest but Mrs S went over to the baby, swaddled her in a fluffy towel and brought her over to me. She was beautiful but so pale, so still. I unwound the fluffy towel she was wrapped in and counted her little toes and fingers. They were purple, although her face was pale, and they felt cold. Then I cried and my tears ran onto her little face. It was such a wonderful feeling that I had given birth to this little being, yet so indescribably sad. The nurse made as if to take her away but Mrs S pushed her off and, while the doctor looked at her, he nodded and she brought over a little bonnet I'd knitted and put it on over the patch of black, black hair, and wrapped the lacy shawl over the fluffy towel. The infant had no look of Kris and that hair colour was as black as my brothers'.

'Have a cuddle of your babby, my dear, have a cuddle…and wait a minute…' She ran to my cupboard and in a few seconds was back with my Box Brownie.

The nurse tut-tutted at this but Doctor Soames put out his arm.

'You go ahead, young lady.'

Mrs S leaned over my shoulder and took a couple of photographs of little Avril. I kissed the tiny, smooth and oh so chilled little brow. She was so perfect.

Doc Soames came over, took my pulse then took her from me, very gently. 'I'm sorry, my dear, so very, very sorry, but I must take her now. She was stillborn, you see, and it's not allowed that I let her stay.'

Reverend P came to the other side of me, made the sign of the cross on my own forehead and whispered, 'She has been baptised and will rest in consecrated ground, my dear. At my church. I'll see to it. You can come and see later. Now rest easy and recover.'

They all left and I was left too. With nothing. That's a horrible word being 'left'.

Mrs S came back in my room holding the little camera. 'With this you'll have witness to your memories, little lass, and all will be done properly and perfectly. Now, here's a big pill the doctor's left for you, to help you sleep. I'll be downstairs. I'll stay, don't worry. Just call me if you need me.'

I squeezed her hand and then I think I drifted off.

Thursday, 26 March

I woke to bright daylight. Hours had passed. I turned over in bed and something stung and pulled a bit, so I yelped. The door opened and in came a young lass in a blue nurse's uniform. I didn't want to talk; she indicated to me she'd bring me some breakfast soon but first I was to be freshened up and did I have any pain and soreness. She wasn't all starchy like the last one and, at my timid nod, she asked me to lie still as she ministered to me. I felt as if it wasn't happening, that it had all been a dream, but I rubbed my hand over my flat stomach area and then I knew. I couldn't speak, I was so choked with emotion.

Blue Nurse positively encased me in stretchy bandages, smiled at her handiwork then announced she would shortly be bringing up a boiled egg that Mrs Smiles was preparing for me; that Mrs S would then go home to see if everything was all right and would return and make a milky drink for me. Or would I prefer a cup of tea straight away? She talked on, and I nodded when it seemed necessary. I was instructed to lie back and rest. Everything was under control. It was happening. It was all organised. It was unreal.

Friday, 27 March

I was certain Uncle W would return today because his boys had to be collected tomorrow, so I dressed properly and have to admit it was a good feeling to squeeze reasonably well into one of my own dresses. I went downstairs for breakfast, feeling quite hungry. Mrs Smiles looked at me a little shyly as if she didn't know how to greet me, so I went over and gave her a big hug.

'Aye now, lass, sit down and let's get ready to face the day. Strictly speaking, you should still be in bed, recovering, but at least sit down and let me fix things hereabouts while you talk. I think it's good that you're up an' walkin'. You'll have heard that telephone thing ring – it was your uncle and he'll be on the afternoon train. I didn't tell him about the little babby of course. That's not my job, miss.'

It's now almost two o'clock and my uncle will be here soon. How will he react to my news? Will he be relieved? Will he have any sympathy for me? On a practical note, I can now seek employment, find an occupation and not have to support a child. That will reassure him to some extent. Also, as there is now no evidence of my misdemeanour, can I persuade him to agree not to tell the family?

The possibility of deceiving my mother in this way was abhorrent to me. Before the birth, I had thought that the knowledge of a grandchild would delight her and lessen any upset. Now there is an event to relate but it would make no difference to her; she would still be uncommonly distressed and bound to tell my father. I doubt if he would allow me back under his roof, he can be so rigid in his principles; much as I love him, I feel his condemnation – and it would be no less – would cause my mum incalculable distress. Oh dear, what was that saying in that book on Uncle's library shelf? Oh yes…it was *Marmion* written by Walter Scott: 'oh what a tangled web we weave when first we practise to deceive'. Well, Katherine Beatrice, that fits you perfectly. Now you have to find ways to seek redemption.

Later that day: Uncle W literally breezed in. I'd been lying on my bed, but at least I was dressed.

He had obviously been told. 'I'm so sorry, my dear girl, I really am, that you had to face such an ordeal without family around you. Are you feeling…ahem…comfortable? Are you not too soon walking around? Seems hard to appreciate what you have so recently suffered.'

I sat up, sideways, feet on the floor. He actually walked over and gave me a big smoky-smelling hug, like people always smell when they've been on a train. I had steeled myself to face him and his very niceness broke me up. I blubbed all over his waistcoat for quite a few minutes while he stroked my hair.

'Now now, Katherine, the worst is over. Don't distress yourself any further. Come, let's sit and we can exchange stories.'

The last thing I wanted was more talk of me and the infant. 'Uncle, did you see Rosie at all?'

He literally beamed at me. 'I did, and she passed her audition with flying colours, I believe. She's to be the second understudy for one of the daughters in the show – Klarchen, or something like that. Did you know she can sing, Katherine?'

'Sing? No! Goodness, Uncle, that's wonderful. She talked only of her love for dancing, and isn't she in a chorus? It's *The White Horse Inn*, I know, and it's set in Austria but I've never heard Rosie singing. Is she a soprano or contralto?'

'Goodness yourself, niece!' He laughed. 'I don't know one name from another but if I like the sound, well, that's different. Rosalie has been rehearsing quite intensively and she's in the chorus as a regular feature but, if called upon, she needs to know the words of the music. You know, she demonstrated some of her dance steps to me and, oh my goodness, she kicks her legs up into the air, quite showing too much of them above the knees, and she has to wear black suspenders, which are really more suitable kept under a lady's skirts… It's actually termed a musical comedy and opens in the Coliseum on 8 April. Perhaps, if I'm still here, we can go down on the train and see the show. Would you like that?'

'I certainly would, but what do you mean if you're still here?'

He packed his pipe. 'Hmm. Well, you know of Uncle George marrying again? Rosalie and I have been talking. She was a little upset; your Uncle George had written telling her of her new stepmother, rather tactless, I suppose, but she appreciates the fact that he'll have help and company at the farm. Your Aunt Erica's willing to come and live in Adelaide in our Kensington Gardens house so we can be together. And Alicia too, of course. She's ready for high school now and her mother has her eye on a school. I've set the boys up for their education. I believe in girls having the same chances. I guess you understand. So I must look into steamer times and head home. Not in too much of a hurry, though. I want the boys to feel secure first. They'll have this place as their home in hols and whenever they want it, but it all needs working out. Above all, my dear, you must feel free to come home with me. I shall happily pay your fare and you can take up your place at training college. You may be late joining but that's no handicap, is it?'

This was all announced between noisy puffs on his pipe. The smell was not unpleasant, smelled of cherries, I thought, but the smoke irritated my eyes. I sat, channelling my thoughts, as he tackled his pipe. Teaching, training college, seemed so strange, almost alien concepts. Yet only months ago…

He seemed to sense my hesitation. 'You take your time to decide, Katherine. Do know this: unless you wish to tell any in the family of your recent experience, of the baby and everything, it will not be made known by me. It may seem hard but I now feel no obligation to tell your mother. She's my sister and I know the division, unpleasantness, the news might cause between her and Frank and maybe some others. Let's keep it as your secret, my dear, yours to tell if and when you wish. Unless something untoward happens… That's how I see it.'

I ran over to him and, pipe and all, gave him a big hug. 'Thank you more than I can say for your understanding, Uncle, and your forgiveness. I would like to take time to consider your offer if I may.' Then, tears welling yet again, I ran from the room.

I ran out into the back garden, realising how much I'd stayed indoors over the last fortnight or so, sewing and reading and knitting and generally feeling worried about myself. There were some lovely spring flowers popping up on the borders, I noticed – some like white daffodils, new to me. I bent down to smell and a voice came from over the low, privet hedge separating our garden from the neighbour's.

'Doctor doesn't encourage lying in then, Miss Symonds? I suppose it's the modern way.' She smiled and waved a watering can up high to demonstrate what she was about.

This must be the Mrs Graham Uncle William and Aunt Erica first met when they both lived here years ago. I'd seen her at a distance before, but not to speak. She's a tall woman with dark brown hair tied back, looks to be in her late forties perhaps. A pleasantly low voice.

I walked to the hedge over the wet lawn and held out my hand. 'Oh, I'm not Miss Symonds, I'm Katherine, Katherine Flack. Mr Symonds is my mother's brother and a dear uncle.' He deserves the accolade, bless him, perhaps more than I deserve him.

She clasped my extended hand. 'I know your little baby died, Katherine – if I may call you Katherine? I sometimes feel myself that if all is not well, the good Lord takes his own steps...'

Well, I realised she was being kind but I didn't want to talk about baby Avril now. 'Thank you. I believe you're Mrs Graham?'

She gave a gracious nod and a brown curl fell over her brow. Her hand withdrew to tuck it back into place. 'I met your uncle first a few years ago, and his lady wife, when they were here and working on the garden for a while. Then when Mrs Symonds was expecting they decided to ship home to have the baby born Australian. And they were babies, plural, now old enough to sail back to come to their father's old school. My, how time flies.'

I was about to turn back to the house when I heard a voice saying, 'Aunt Liz, do introduce me.' A girl in a greenish school uniform and white blouse came over to the fence, extending her hand to me; it was rather ink-stained.

I smiled, took it and gave it a firm shake.

She too had a pleasantly low-toned voice. 'I'm Edna, just home from school.'

She looked to be about thirteen or fourteen, but as tall as her aunt. 'It's nice to meet you. Aunt Liz tells me I met your aunt and uncle when they were here before. I was little more than a baby because when I saw your uncle the other day I didn't recognise him. Isn't that rude of me!' She laughed. 'He said you were going to be a teacher. My mother's a teacher. She'll be at school till late tonight, that's why I'm here.'

Her aunt patted her arm. 'Come on, my lass. We have soup to warm up. You can show me how good you are at laying a table. Goodbye, Katherine. Do come round any time for tea and scones – my usual time is three o'clock.'

And off they went.

Saturday, 28 March

Well, journal, I was a bit quiet yesterday but meeting Mrs Graham and her niece was a happy few minutes. I have a lot of thinking to do. It worries me a little bit that I'm not so keen to return home as I thought I would be. Is it guilt? I don't know but I'm not happy at deceiving my mother. Perhaps it's because I want to see more of England while I'm here. It'll be a number of weeks before we go, or Uncle W goes, or whoever, so there's time to visit Rosie and see her show and…well, other things.

I went for a walk down Beastbanks again, just enjoying the sunshine. Didn't buy much. Uncle W's driven to Windermere to collect his boys, so Mrs Smiles is all cheerful bustling around the house. Annoyingly, she won't let me do too much but I've told her that the boys when they arrive must not be given any clues about the baby – their father's orders.

I came home to see a note for me from young Edna of next door, inviting me to tea tomorrow because it's her thirteenth birthday. Nice to be invited and, despite having a baby, perhaps I still look only seventeen. Yet I feel so much older. I feel at least ten years older. Deciding I'd best find her a present – chocolates perhaps – I toddled back down the hill. I'd earlier noticed this little sweet shop at the bottom of the hill with a faded window display mainly of soaps and laundry powders.

Inside, the shopkeeper seemed overwhelmed just to have a possible customer – so overwhelmed she nearly dropped her knitting! 'Sorry, madam. Doorbell's bust an' I can't fix it.'

I smiled and made my way over to a small display of boxed chocolates on her counter and selected six large and luscious fruit chocolates in a pretty, painted box. Inscribed on the lid in a decorative script was 'Mitson's, artists in chocolate'.

'Them's med in Nottingham, madam. Way sooth o' Kendal.'

I was almost tempted myself but I really want to regain some of my original shape.

The shopkeeper gave me a paper bag in which to carry the box and, as she pressed her till keys, told me, 'Money's tight an' I've more fowk just lookin' in't winder and wishin' than comes in and wants service. Good day to you, madam.'

I felt quite ridiculously guilty. I thought deeply about this world depression crisis as I walked back up the hill. I'd been so concerned with my own situation, how I feel and what I should do, I'd quite disregarded the implications for all the folk around me. Uncle W is well-heeled, I know, and he didn't lose as much as he might have – his words – when the bubble burst. Wasn't that in America last year or the year before? I remember Mum telling me of his relief and how he could afford to bring us all to England with him.

I stopped suddenly as I realised what a good turn he'd done for me, though he didn't know it then. My dad…he'd have chased Kris to Melbourne to give him what for and probably insisted we married. Ugh. I renewed my walk up the hill. Here I'm free from such restrictions

– I'm quite sure Kris did not plan to be saddled with a wife so early – and thanks to Uncle W my reputation is intact. Then I realised I've yet to tell Mum about my pregnancy, the baby. How do I do that? It'll kill her! Dad will bring on that cold anger of his and the Schmidts will victimise him and they'll blame me because even Ralph warned me about Kris so I should have known more than I did and…

I sat down on the wooden bench by the side of the road to catch my breath. By the time I set off back up the hill, I knew I had to ask Uncle W's advice – and maybe his help.

Sally

18

Oh, wow! Katherine wrote about the experience in such detail; guess it was just such a hugely stirring experience she couldn't not record it. It's in such a chatty format I wonder if it's meant to read as a novel? Eventually? Or perhaps she wanted a record whose accuracy she could rely on later, so she could confess or let us, her inheritors (is that the word?) know what happened. Or, so well hidden as it's been all these years, was it intended only to be read after her death? Did she ever confess to her mother? Her Uncle William knew, and that Doctor Elena; did anyone else? My mother would have mentioned had she known and certainly that little photo of Avril meant little to her. Did my dad know he might have had had a half-sister? It seems not. Poor Dad.

Poor, poor Granny Kath. I feel incredibly sad. For whatever reason, she felt she could not confide in anyone – well, no one of her own family. She suffered on her own and later in life, never allowing anyone else to know her secret. I find it hard to understand that it was then considered such a sinful act that she could not allow her father to know; worse, her mother, because she would have told her father and there would have been wider-ranging unpleasantness. Was the sin because the families were friends, allies in the church? Or was it that girls had to keep themselves for marriage only to their husband? Life was then bound by rules, it seems to me, rules made by men and remarkably hypocritical!

Seems so unlikely now, here in the twenty-first century where single-parent families – usually a mother – receive financial benefits and certainly a measure of understanding. No longer is there the sting of disgrace, victimisation, or isolation from family and friends. Opinions are expressed, yes, but we're nowadays more tolerant – if only for the sake of the child. And this happened to Katherine long before her younger sister was ostracised by her family because of her transgression, and that must have been made known to her. Ostensibly, she learned of Jacinta's death the day her little Samuel took the telegram. Did she know the children were being fostered by her twin brother and his wife? I wonder, did Granny never mention that to Mum? Jacinta was her younger sister after all. So much was hidden, so much deceit. Oh, what a tangled web we weave when first we practise to deceive. It rings through my brain; this is Katherine's web.

I don't think I can tell my mother about Katherine's sinning. I rather feel she's wanting something of the sort to come out of all this paperwork and I feel she would positively relish the news! Does that sound mean of me?

Later that evening and this is so hard to comprehend – the coincidence, well, it knocked me for six. Where's James when I need him? I checked my Facebook notification and clicked on a message from an Annette Summers. She wrote how her daughter Melanie is 'always on Facebook when she should be doing her homework! But for once I'm quite pleased or I would not have heard from you. My grandmother's name was Jacinta Flack, my mother was Irene and she became a Simms. Unfortunately she has Alzheimers and she's unable to recognise anyone, so I don't recommend you visiting. Does anyone else in the family have beautiful red hair? Nan Irene had lovely auburn hair, I have dark brown but Melanie's is a glorious red! I would like to meet up some time if we can arrange it. Let's keep in touch.'

Well well well…

Katherine

19

Sunday, 29 March 1931

Palm Sunday. It was good hearing all the boy's experiences at their school, they chatted on until quite late last night. This morning was no quieter over breakfast but Mrs Smiles was delighted at the boys' appetites, and Uncle W was in seventh heaven with his boys around him. They're lovely lads, as Mrs Smiles says often, too often! Maybe so, but I was glad to escape later to next door.

Goodness but what steep steps, seven of them, up to their front door. The party was to be in Aunt Liz's house, not where Edna lives, which I gather is a few streets away. I was expected at 3 p.m. because the senior Grahams were off to church for the morning Palm Sunday service. I was met at the door by a very pompous man, waistcoat, watch chain and all. He actually greeted me and then shook my hand, (so modern) saying he was so pleased to meet me.

'I met your uncle first when they lived here before, m'dear. Lovely wife, too. Well, come in out of the draught, do.'

Turns out to be Uncle Frank. 'Graham Senior, m'dear, as the Americans say. We have a son Frank, too. He's away at the moment.'

Then Edna came running out from the drawing room. 'Hello again. Do come in and meet my mam.'

Mam – not Mum – was another tall, angular woman, about my mother's age. She too shook my hand, introducing herself as Mary Peach. She then persuaded from behind her, where he'd been gripping her skirt, a little boy with a shock of gloriously auburn hair. He looked to be about five or six and was terribly bashful, so I pretended to ignore him.

Then he looked up at me and said, 'I'm Georgie.'

I smiled. I'm accepted!

So were the chocolates.

Edna's mother seemed quite emotional. 'Oh, I know their shop and factory. It was down Mansfield Road, Lenton area. That was near where we lived in Nottingham.' She smiled. 'I hope the birthday girl will let me have a taste for old time's sake!'

Judging by the birthday girl's grin, I thought she would.

The mum, Mrs Peach, commented how Mrs Briggs would have been delighted to make a sale and that led on to an adult discussion about the national economy. Mr Graham, it seems, is the district bank manager, and oversees every Midland Bank in the county. I thought how they were, as a family, obviously financially comfortable. Mr Graham said that Britain's unemployment has now exceeded two million! He felt passionately for the men who'd fought in the war and made it home again only to face financial hardship.

It was interesting to listen to his discussion with his wife and Mrs P how he had instructed some house payments, mortgages owed to the bank, to be given extended time as much and as often as possible to those men who had been made redundant through no fault of their own. From what he said, he had the authority to also reduce the mortgagee's interest rate. Such power! He believed ex-soldiers deserved to be settled with work and making a family and every one should be helped to retain his home and his self-respect as long as possible. Also, through the bank, he had instigated a number of new-start land-buying schemes for soldier settlers.

I was fascinated, listening; felt sorry I'd thought him pompous. I also understood how he and Uncle W had been friends and now understood why they have an active social conscience; Uncle W's battles on behalf of owner/renters' legal rights back in Australia, particularly for widow women.

I spoke of this to Mr Graham – of Uncle's dedicated battles for the rights of war widows in our state. Some had in-laws wanting their dead soldier sons' and brothers' properties repossessed by the families; the widows, even with children to care for, being often – and conveniently – considered unfit, incapable of maintenance because of small brains (!) to inherit valuable property. We had quite a discussion on legalities versus justice.

I learned that Edna's father had been injured in the war and was a postman now. They'd moved up to Kendal, where Mr Graham managed to find him the postman's work when Mrs Peach was posted to the school. Mr Peach lost a big part of one leg or a muscle or something and the exercise from riding on the post office bicycle had been his salvation, declared Mrs Peach. He couldn't be with us today because, although it was Sunday, he had parcels and other things to sort through before early tomorrow.

I was fascinated listening to all their conversation; it was so different from all my own home life in Hahndorf and here. What the average working man and woman have to endure made me wonder how Edna could even be given a birthday party.

It wasn't extravagant, though; just the usual eats, plus some jelly and fairy cakes with homemade lemonade proudly exhibited by Edna. I was invited to talk about Australia. Strangely, it wasn't easy; I felt as if I had to brush away layers of fog in my head all connected to me and baby Avril and my own personal trouble. They knew about Sydney and the new Harbour Bridge all finished and told me what was in their newspaper, that a renegade captain called de Groot slashed the official tape before the premier could cut it! They knew about Anna Pavlova dying and I said how Rosie was so upset. Mrs Peach had been upset too.

Then Mrs Graham spoke of her sadness at Dame Nellie Melba's death. 'She had the most glorious voice. I listened to her once on the wireless. I saw in the paper that Sir Landon Ronald said in London that hers was the most glorious voice put into the throat of a woman – it was of amazing purity and golden liquidity.'

Of course I knew of Melba and also that she was buried at Lilydale in Victoria. Uncle W had been almost inconsolable when he heard she had died. He told me about Sir Landon Ronald – I'm never surprised at how much of anything at all my uncle knows! It turns out that Sir L was Melba's accompanist on her tours through America and Canada and now has been offered the job as conductor at the Royal Albert Hall Orchestra.

I had to interject. 'Uncle William says he'll take me down to London to see my cousin Rosie and we'll certainly get to a concert, though I don't know which one, at the Albert Hall. I'm so excited.'

There was lots of chat between Georgie and Edna and her two friends from school and I joined more in the adult conversation, listening particularly when Mrs Peach spoke of her school and of a pending vacancy for a classroom assistant teacher. She's concerned that with all the jobless and people so desperately needing work, they'll be flooded with undesirable applicants.

Then I realised that she meant a certain level of education was needed and she'd be hard put to find anyone suitable. My ears twitched and my brain jangled as I helped tidy up afterwards in the kitchen while the girls – the two girls from Edna's school were playing snap with the little boy Georgie – and I asked just what qualifications an assistant teacher needed. It seemed that the position was similar to a probationary nurse, learning on the job. I worked up enough courage to ask if I might meet the criteria and later, sitting around the teapot, I outlined my education so far.

Mrs Peach wasn't the principal but had written much of the curriculum – making sure girls had the same chances as boys was how she described it. It ended up that she'd check with the headmaster, a Mr Sutton, to see if my education was enough for the position.. Her school was called the Central School and was on All Hallow's Lane but despite its name wasn't associated with any of the local churches. It was a higher-grade elementary school and most students left there at age fourteen or fifteen to work.

It seemed she had earlier taught at an elementary school in Nottingham, called High Pavement School, and for a short period had actually made principal. I exclaimed how that was surely a marvellous achievement and she laughed, in a self-deprecating way, saying it was only because all the men were then abroad in the war. Honestly, journal! Couldn't she be straightforward and say she was good enough and that was a just reward?

Now I'm back in my room and writing this and hoping something may come of my showing interest for a position. If so, I may be able to stay in Kendal for up to a year and earn money, see something of the countryside and then perhaps sail home in time to take up a place at the teachers college. Mum should be happy because I'll have attained the magical eighteen years she regards as adult enough to leave home! Adult: huh, what a laugh. The induction to adulthood: have a baby.

I've just been crying my eyes out; now going to bed.

20

Monday, 20 April 1931

Just starting my second week as a classroom assistant. I feel as if it's all a new start. It's been a busy couple of weeks or so. Uncle W and I have been to London on the train to see Rosie at the Coliseum in *The White Horse Inn*. It was great fun to listen to and watch and I saw all around her lodgings and met some of the other girls in the chorus. Rosie is second understudy to one of the main characters, Klarchen (?). Rosie didn't do any singing but later in her digs she and the first understudy girl gave me and Uncle W a concert. Rosalie can sing!

On the Thursday night when the first understudy was on call in the wings, Rosie had the night off and we three went to the Royal Albert Hall.

Rosie asked me how I'd managed to lose the weight then said,

'Ah well, living up those Beastbanks, it's not surprising!'

Does she think I sprint up and down that hill daily? I left her with her thoughts.

Disappointingly, the Albert Hall was being used for a group called the Health and Beauty League and was a demonstration of graceful fitness movements by women. We didn't stay long. Uncle said there would be other opportunities.

However. great relief for me, journal, On arriving home, I find a letter from Doc Elena! The envelope was white, had pencilled scribblings out over the address and red stripes around it, and the stamp had been torn off. 'By a collector,' mused Uncle W.

Doc Elena was in a town called Nowy Krakow, in Slawno in the Western Voivodeship. I think that's right; it was hard to read. She has met up with some old friends of her family and they want her to stay: they have such need of doctors. So she isn't planning a prompt return to England. She actually said she hopes to meet up with me back in Australia maybe next year or the one after. In the meanwhile, if I write to the address given, she might be able to receive the letter, as the post was improving. She said there are many Jewish people in the area and they're nervous of this man called Hitler in Germany, who is campaigning for power. Then, almost as an afterthought, she asked how I was feeling because by now I would have a new baby taking up my time. Dear Doc Elena, I owe her much.

I read parts of the letter to Uncle W.

'Goodness me, Uncle! I'll write to her with some of our news this very evening. We hear more of this man Hitler in this country, too, do we not? That Oswald Mosely here is a great admirer of him, isn't he?'

Uncle W's reaction was to turn down his lip and shake his head. Oops, let's say no more. He did caution me against reciting any German language in my school activities because feeling is building politically and this Mr Hitler is the catalyst, so he pronounced angrily.

I haven't followed much in the newspapers. I've been tired on returning home each afternoon. I don't have higher-level marking to do like accredited teachers have, but I've a lot of reading prescribed for me, mainly by Mrs Peach. She's very particular about certain points in assessing the students' work.

I'm not allowed to mark the maths papers but she recognises my writing skills and allows me to assess the written essays. They have quite long papers to write once a calendar month and she sets them for the following month as she collects the ones completed. She likes the pupils not to vary from the topic, but to research it as thoroughly as they're able and for two hours on a Wednesday morning it's my task to take a class or a group of students across the senior classes to the Carnegie Library in Stricklandgate.

It's not a long walk down there and I like to listen to the chat of the pupils as we walk along. The library is an impressive building, opened in 1909 – a plaque says so, and the words 'Let there be Light' are prominently above the front door. That phrase really kindles in me a wish to learn more and work up to a responsible position. I have to keep the students close to me but I do find time to choose books for myself to read, and to return the previous borrows.

I've written back to Doc Elena too, telling her of the baby dying, that she was christened and that she's buried in a grassy corner of the church yard dedicated to stillborns. They don't have individual memorials but there's a huge chunk of slate under a tree that's engraved with the words 'Suffer the Little children…' The sentence is incomplete but somehow it's enough and it's comforting. I met the Reverend Paulus there one day and he directed me to it. He has sympathetic eyes and I'm sure he feels the sadness of a loss, though he himself has, so Mrs Smiles tells me, eleven, yes eleven (!), children of his own. I told Doc E most of the Avril story and I've asked her to still keep it secret, as Uncle W and I have agreed that is the best way. I cannot bear the thought of upsetting my mum, and I know she'll take the news badly. If I ever find the courage to confess.

Friday, 19 June

There's a shocking cattle disease here and farmers aren't allowed to move cattle – or it seems, any other animal – to markets, just in case. It's called foot and mouth disease. That means that milk is in very short supply. But farmers are now losing money and with the shocking unemployment figures in this country – 2.66 millions I read in the paper – schoolchildren are suffering not only from lack of milk but also because their parents are even more short of money for food than before. It is so depressing, journal.

Uncle's made a booking to sail home to check on his own and Aunt Erica's affairs. The liner is the SS *Strathnaver* and he's booked to Melbourne via Bombay and Colombo. That's forty days travel; continuing to Sydney would take forty-two. Only tourist-class space left – more than half the spaces are tourist level apparently – so he'll be sharing a cabin with someone he doesn't know. Funny Uncle, I suspect he's modest – yet he shared as a young man in school and then at Oxford University. I wonder if they'll set up in the Adelaide house again, and for how long. His boys are staying here so surely they'll be coming back sometime. He admits to me he just doesn't know what's waiting for him over there; he's really worried about his brother, that's Uncle George, taking a new wife and whether her children may inherit the property later.

Well, he's a lawyer, I'm sure he'll sort things out to his satisfaction, but I do hope he comes back here while I'm still here! I shall miss him. Is that selfish of me, journal?

Tuesday, 1 September

It's my mother's birthday today; she'll be fifty, I think. She seems older than that in my mind. I embroidered a handkerchief for her and Uncle will post it from Melbourne or Adelaide to her – though he hopes to see her too. He should be almost at Melbourne by now. It'll be strange for his boys, his not being here between school terms.

As Mrs S reminded me, 'You'll be here, won't yer, luv? Yer on't holidays thisen.'

The implication was obvious – anything other than maintenance is my responsibility. Ah well, as long as I can get to the library and maybe to the cinema, I'll be fine. Nick and Steve came here over a week ago and so far they're very little trouble. They had Mrs Smiles delighted because – and this is the school boarding house routine – they make up their beds and hang their clothes away properly every day. And she really enjoys ironing their shorts! I insist on ironing my things, though; she's a dear but has bad feet – standing to press acres of fabric is no good for her. I make sure we all eat together at dinnertime, or teatime as Mrs S calls it, and that way I hope I'm keeping up with their activities.

This last I've kept in mind because *Frankenstein* is showing at the Palladium and that should be the kind of film they'd enjoy, so I suggested it last night and they're off to see it with the vicar's eldest boy this evening; he's sixteen and quite a serious fellow, but honourable I'm sure. Concerning me, there are two full weeks of break! I wrote some time ago to see if Rosie would like to come up and stay, me being on holiday also, but she hasn't answered. As far as I know, she's still in London but apparently, according to Uncle W from when he was in London, she had chances of joining an amateur touring theatre company for the off season. He reported her optimism to me and that she'll be receiving a wage, and that accommodation is usually cheap for these tourers. She had told him how she was looking forward to travelling around the country and seeing different towns.

I know, journal, that I've grumbled about her in the past but I really miss news of her, and even herself! She seems to have disappeared. I'm sure she would have written or even telephoned had she left the city though. Yes, journal, I wrote to Mum for her birthday; have to allow about a month and I did, so I hope she knows I remembered.

21

Sunday, 4 October 1931

Letter from my mother thanking me for my birthday greetings only two days late and she was pleased I'd remembered it was her fiftieth. Uncle W was driving up to Hahndorf the following afternoon and phoned her to say I've sent her a little gift; he'll give it to her personally. Lovely.

She wrote that Papa had made her a carved bedroom chair with rolled legs and the backboard carved with a heart intertwined with very recognisable wild flowers. She was enraptured! She also said the twins had liked their birthday letters and especially the English pound note placed in each envelope! Arthur asked how much his pound was worth in Australia because he knows that the Bank of England devalued the pound sterling. He took his to the bank in the high street to ask how many Australian shillings it was now worth! Jacinta wants to put her pound note into a frame and she'll paint something English around it.

I so like hearing about the twins; I do miss them. Jacinta appears to be a handful, though; Mum says she wants to learn French not German because she wants to travel the world and, to her, lingua franca implies a seniority in languages! Then she and her friend Mona decided to find out about animal reproduction; they each knew of dogs having pups, nothing new there, but they contrived a plan; they drove some of Laubsch's ewes into his chicken pen, which happened to be near the sheep yard where his prize ram was waiting for the vet to come and fix a cracked horn. Well, the ram sensed the ewes, the ewes ran to and from the ram and, in Jacinta's words, a most unholy tangle of epithets burst forth from Mr Laubsch. The vet managed to restrain the ram, but Mr Laubsch brought his epithets to the joinery too, demanding Papa go round to the Laubsch's and fix his chicken-wire fence. All Jacinta said – in no way an apology – was 'The ram's a fool for missing an opportunity.'

Apparently, on reaching sixteen, her twin Arthur has decided he wants to be an artist and from the end of this school year take formal lessons from Miss Nora at the Cedars. After that at the School of Fine Arts in North Adelaide, like Nora did. Papa Frank insists that Arthur must complete his final year of school but has compromised in that the boy can attend Sallie Heysens's classes at the Cedars on weekends. As Katherine knows, says Mum, Aunt Evie studied there for years and even now is still selling her works. Mum thinks Aunt Evie, his sister, persuaded Papa to adopt this compromise. She told her brother that study from a professional would help Arthur in his precision drawing, and that may come in handy at the master joinery.

Clever Aunt Evie, journal. I do agree. And as I read all these titbits from home, I do feel homesick. It's almost the time of year that I should be thinking of going home, looking up sailing times of the big ships. I need to be enrolled at the teachers college pretty soon, even though classes won't begin till next March. I know how to organise it all, Uncle W left me the name of his contact in the shipping office. I also know what a good feeling it is helping young people learn; leading them in a class, imparting ideas – all that is part of teaching and I could learn to do it well, I know. It's just that I've been uncertain about meeting up with Mum, knowing how I deceived her. Can I live there, day after day, knowing? And what if Kris S learns I'm back and comes to see me? What do I say? Nothing? Oh, what a tangled web we weave when first we practise to deceive.

I think I might wait a while to write to Mum in Hahndorf. It's so hard not to burst out with my news about the baby but if I did, that would be nothing less than Armageddon. Mum would have to carry the burden of Dad's fury. I cannot allow that.

Sunday, 11 October

I've just heard on the wireless that Australia's great General Sir John Monash is being buried today after lying in state for a couple of days in Melbourne. Papa used to speak of him with great admiration, so I guess did many Aussies, including Uncle W. I wonder how he's getting on, by the way, with all his house-moving activities. Won't be easy for Aunt Erica. She'll miss her surgery work in Renmark. They had tenants in the Adelaide house who would need to vacate so I estimate they'll still be at Cumquats, the Renmark property.

Yes, journal, tomorrow I shall contact the shipping agent. I might even write to Mum. I've not answered her last one yet. But when I know I can take a ship, I'll ask her to enrol me in the teachers training college. I do so miss them all and one thing I've learned, with all the help I've received over her, with all the experience gained in the Central School thanks to Mrs Peach, is that I do want to be a teacher and rise to the top of my tree.

Mrs Peach says Mr Sutton is pleased with me and considers me at the least as good a teacher as some who've come to the school with diplomas. He'll be happy to write me a testimonial to take home with me. He says he won't replace me yet, though, but will wait until I can give him a date. People are so good!

Thursday, 5 November

I picked up the *Gazette* today and sure enough it reported on the Melbourne Cup, held on the 3rd, and – goodness me – Phar Lap was unplaced. I imagine Uncle W will be pleased – he always claimed it was never a good idea to pick the favourite. Bet he made some money but I've no idea about the other horses and of course they're mentioned – other than the winner, very unromantically named White Nose.

Ahah…I hear the letter box clattering. It's about time the steamship company let me know of a likely sailing…they do take their time.

Later. The clattering was a note from Edna, asking if I'd like to go with them to some place where the bonfire's been built and there's a Guy on top of it – all to be burnt because of the failed plot to burn down the Houses of Parliament back in whichever century it was. I declined; it's a wet and miserable morning and I doubt if the rain will clear before tonight. I don't have any lessons today at the school; because of the Guy Fawkes celebrations the pupils have the afternoon off and I think I'll use my free time to write a letter back to Mum. I've owed her a reply for some time.

Even later…tucked up in bed I am at the moment and just closed my window. We're quite high up here and I can see the glow over to the east, I think, where the bonfire is still smouldering. It must have been enormous. I can certainly smell the smoke of it, despite the drizzly weather. I can just imagine all the chatter in the classes tomorrow about it. Edna said there would be fireworks too, but I think they must have been before I stood at the window. I'm sure she enjoyed herself!

Saturday, 7 November

The Saturday post and I am dead, d.e.a.d. Uncle W has written (and I only posted one off to him a couple of days ago) but I am dead, journal. To all parties. Everyone who matters in my life. Uncle W tells me that he shared my secret with Aunt Erica and she was most upset but *for* me, not *at* me. (She is a doctor, after all.) However, Uncle George was sitting on the stairs – he apparently often does to smoke his pipe – and he overheard. So Uncle W confessed and said it must be kept secret and Mum, over in Hahndorf, must not hear of it. But George was furious and said how everyone always took a swipe at his daughter Rosalie because of what Aunt Erica calls her music hall lifestyle and now it seems that I, the saint of the family, have committed such a sin! He told Uncle W that if he didn't tell Mum, he would, that Mum is their big sister and she's owed that much. Apparently, says Uncle W, Uncle G then actually telephoned her.

Mum then insisted on chastising Uncle W in no uncertain terms and so he and Erica agreed that I must know that my sin is no longer a secret.

Oh, dear God, what happens now! My mum knows. She'll feel honour bound to tell Dad. Dad will rant and rave or, even worse, clamp his mouth shut and go out into his workshop and be quietly furious as he decides what to say, or do. So do I put pen to paper straight away and admit my sin and make some reason for the deceit – somehow – one they may accept out of love for me…or…?

Monday, 9 November

I wrote a good number of first pages to Mum and haven't posted any. This morning came one from Rosie and, journal, I was almost too scared to open it. She was writing from Portsmouth. She's in some am dram group that tours around and at least it's work over the bad season, so she says. No mention of my baby, or of what I've done or not done, and in a way that's a relief. She's not coming here for Christmas though; she's sailing home!

I'm flabbergasted. My agent keeps telling me he has no places due to the military taking over a number of ships to turn them into troop ships – a mystery in itself – but Rosie cops a berth! Well, I know I'm offering only to pay third class and maybe she has more money. I must telephone her. No, I can't, I don't know her number, but I can ask off the exchange, so I'll see. I might telephone my travel fellow and find out what's what, although even as I write this journal I wonder if I'll ever be welcome at home?

Rosie doesn't say why she's going back; unusual for her if she has a success or something blissful (her word) waiting for her. She's going to Melbourne then taking the train to Renmark. Probably wants to meet this new stepmother. I know I would.

My parents are a different kettle of fish and Dad can be so unbending. Ralph will be even worse, I imagine, yet it was his friend who fathered Avril. Does make me think if Ralph and Kris's sister… ah well, don't really care. I know that because of me there'll be ructions between Mum and Dad and possibly an unhappy situation pervading throughout the whole joinery. O merciful heaven…

Had a sick girl to care for in school today. She had to stay in school, too young and too sick to go home when her mother's not there, and Mrs Peach said her mother would get the sack from her job if she wanted time off and that can't happen because the father's lost his job already and they only have the one income and that's barely enough to live on, said Mrs P. And fathers don't look after sick children of course; they need to go to the exchange and wait to be hired for labouring.

Wednesday, 11 November, Remembrance Day

It used to be Armistice Day. No school today, though, and I didn't write anything yesterday so can catch up today. No postal service today of course. I had to mark some grammar pages for Mrs P, who trusts me, and she was sick. I'm feeling sick myself but it's all down to suspense about when Mum will write to me. I know she will, it's just what she'll say that scares me. And I'm scared to book a ship, even if the agent tells me of a place. If I don't, what will I do?

Mrs P is sick also; she probably caught the thing that other students seem to be going down with. Usually, Mrs P blames the predominance of potatoes when the students are sick; they all seem to live on nothing else, or so she says. I don't know why more families don't have a little garden and grow green stuff. I mentioned this and she said how her sister, my next-door neighbour, plants trays of cabbage seedlings which Mrs P gives out to various groups from the classes.

Next morning

IT CAME. The letter from Mum I've been expecting. The envelope was wet and made of such thin paper anybody could see through it. Rain, rain and more rain here. I stood, holding it, scared to read what I was sure it'd say. I carried it to school with me and didn't open it till I reached the cloakroom. I should have waited – it's such an angry letter, journal. More than just mad, it's so bitter it doesn't seem like Mum writing it. The writing's scrawled all over the page and I know Mum wrote it as soon as she heard my news, not thinking of anything other than how she felt.

There's no date on it but worst thing ever, journal, she says I needn't hurry to come home. Oh, dear God, what does that mean? I'm writing this in my dinner break at twelve o'clock. I want to cry then I feel angry and wonder if Ralph put two and two together and told Kris, and he'll not take any blame, I know that, men never do, and to be fair it was my fault. I really knew what I was not supposed to do but…the bell's ringing. Have to get back into class.

And the next morning

One came from Jazz…oh, er…I think it's written a few days after Mum wrote hers, tells of consequences but only in a few lines, hardly worth the stamp. She's furious with me; says Dad's turned on Mum saying she – Jazz – has to be carefully watched now 'cos Mum was careless with me and it can't be repeated. She adds her embarrassment is excruciating as 'Dad plans to stand up in church and tell of his daughter fallen from Grace and that's you, Katherine, not me!' Then on the other side from where she folded it she writes, 'Dad says don't bother coming home until you are truly repentant and if that's never, it's soon enough!' And that's all emphasised by a multitude of scratchy underlining that in one place actually cut the paper! Oh, my gods… and she calls him not Papa, but Dad. More changes I don't know about – even that hurts.

I sat in the bathroom bawling my eyes out and Mrs Smiles just tut-tutted and told me I'd better get a move on or I'll be late. I'm done, journal, at the end of my tether. So I won't chase up the travel agent, I shall stay here and just exist…

Sally

22

Tuesday, 26 June 2018

Well, it was back around Anzac Day that I last had another look at Granny Kath's papers. I've just fished out that little tooth powder tin that came in the suitcase. It warrants a closer look. Very odd! Traces of pink powder around the base walls but the contents – well!

A very small black and white picture, folded in half and squeezed in the tin at the top. It's of a boy aged about five wearing a belted overcoat, heavy shoes and looks like knitted knee socks. He has a small suitcase strung diagonally over the body. Can't be one of William's boys. Looks foreign. Underneath the pic is a large kirby grip – I think that's what they were called – like a hairslide. Then a minuscule manicure file thing carved in bone, its small pointed digits swivelling on a central pivot; so tiny! A white tablet or pill, screwed in paper, was next; guess this to be a paracetamol or similar, then a half-crown coin dated 1910, a bit flattened; and then – and I had to ease it out with a knife point – a tightly packed and cleverly folded paper note, covered from edge to edge on both sides with the tiniest black ink writing. In French! How could this little tin carry so much? There was a cardboard circle folded in four and below that a six-pointed star with the word *Jude* inked in the centre. It's in a grubby yellowy felted material.

I look and look and I'm cringing inside then engulfed, no lesser word, by an anger I've never known. I want to scream. To hit out. I stand upright, knocking the little tin off my knee onto the carpet. I run out to the rear veranda, onto the pavers and run up and down on the spot, stomp, stamp, stomp, stamp, faster and faster, fasterfasterfaster with fists clenched until I'm out of breath. That one word – who doesn't recognise it and realise what it implied then? I feel actually nauseous so make myself breathe more slowly to walk indoors again, lifting poor Mog up from the carpet with my foot as I do so. I down a glass of cold water then, contrite at treating my cat so rudely, open his own can of kitty dinner in the laundry.

I regain my chair, pick up the tin's contents from the carpet then take a couple of deep breaths. My horror intensifies as I recall my scant knowledge of the history. I'm feeling actually nauseous as I slowly… deliberately…unwrap the cardboard circle. The word *kindertransport,* one long word in Germanic lettering, was around the top rim, something else unintelligible in faded German around the lower edge. Inked in the centre of the circle was a five-digit number in yellowing ink, barely discernible.

Paradox: hot coals in my fingers and a knob of ice in my belly. This cardboard circle is a hastily constructed badge of entitlement. To freedom. Any student of modern history would know of it; the translation is 'children's transport' and it was the means by which thousands of German Jewish and some other European children were able to escape the Nazis, a program that began at the end of 1938.

With a small sharp knife, and a shaking hand, I slowly and carefully extract an edge of the cardboard so tightly folded on the base of the tin. There's a marking, not the clearest. Fudged, been wet at some time; a fingerprint? Why was one needed unless required to give ID? I'd never seen an actual print but they're often on TV police dramas and such shows. I'd never had one taken. It's quite a precision arrangement of whorls, is that the word? But whose? Katherine's? Did she require proof of identity? Why the kirby grip? As a tool and in partnership with the lethal-looking bone manicure set, did she pick locks?

Wow. All this is a surprise. What's next! This suggestion of Katherine's being involved in such a key event in European history has me now in suspense. Certainly doesn't fit too easily with my reminiscences of Granny Kath watching her TV soaps and baking *stollen* or borrowing books for me from her library. Strange tangle of feelings: horror, admiration, and all so horribly unexpected and atypical.

I had been determined to find, pursue Katherine's story but it lacked challenge, mystery, achievement to generate a wider interest, or so I'd been thinking. Nor had I even found any evidence of her making reparation for the weight of guilt she was supposedly carrying – allowing the non sequitur – so valuable to writers. In fiction, the writer can always allow the imagination to run its course (note the success of fantasy novels) but I do like to build on a factual foundation in my stories. Now I'm impatient to learn more, to talk over this new angle with someone who'd listen and suggest… Not Mum, bless her; she'd have it all over her bridge club or the CWA ladies in no time at all.

I quickly riffled through following papers, nothing obvious. So I took pics of the contents to send to James. My mind's working overtime – all conjecture. Need assurance, confirmation – or something. On goes the computer to scan the tiny French writing, both sides, and I forwarded that to him. Oh! How I want to share this with him, to talk, but looking at the clock can see I must be patient. Besides which, their telephone exchange isn't known for its confidentiality; his laptop is in his quarters. I know one of his men is married to a Frenchwoman who used to teach over there; perhaps I could gain a translation.

Well, that will take time. I need to be patient. James had flown home on four-day leave in May for the boys' birthdays but we were busy with family matters for that time. James was highly amused that I'd contacted Facebook to chase descendants of Jacinta's twins. He remembered Granny Kath, or was it my dad, telling him about Jacinta's red hair and, of course, we all then teased Aaron – assuming that's where he inherited his ginger locks. We agreed we'd try and catch up with this far-flung grouping of family – sometime.

We went out for the boys' birthday meal on the 4th; it was a Saturday. Another surprise: Aaron brought a lovely young lass as a guest, one we'd heard him speak of, and he'd brought her home in uni days, but she'd seemed to fade from the scene in later years. Whereas Joanne and Alexander had been together for some time, Aaron had hung out with other young women, some with strange beliefs ranging from unidentifiable religious sects to what James called 'the Earth-Mother-hippy-type'. One he brought home only last Christmas swore like a trooper and admitted to late-onset lesbianism. Apparently her constant use of inventive swear words was her downfall. Thankfully, she didn't last over the New Year! Ariadne and Aaron first met at uni; she was doing first year as his time ended then she stayed on after qualifying to do some tutoring. She's a Fletcher – how that name seems to crop up! She's still working at the uni; I've yet to find out her subjects…

Interesting coincidence, too: her grandparents are from Westmorland in England, where Katherine lived after going there with her Uncle William. I mentioned the connection to her and – wait for it – the Fletchers were in farming and commerce in that area since the year dot! Actually, there are a number of Fletchers around that region, so it's no startling revelation, but it's somehow comforting to recognise the name as having some common origin.

So the boys' celebration became quite a jolly celebration.

It was developed on the Sunday after the birthdays. James had already flown up to Darwin to ship on an advisory mission to Afghanistan. He might not have to go but certainly was involved with the shipping. Such a pity. Aaron and Ariadne announced their engagement. Her parents were pleased and Aaron was relieved. Aaron had whispered in his dad's ear when planning it so I knew James was chuffed. My own antennae sprang upright when Ariadne spoke of her Oz connection from long ago. With the surname Fletcher popping up in Granny Kath's family tree as being the maiden name of her grandmother Beatrice, surely there's a connection?

Beatrice Fletcher cum Beauchamp cum Symonds was Granny Kath's grandmother. Beatrice's father was a Fletcher and he had Fletcher cousins who lived in London then later bought a section of the Fletcher farm when her father married and moved to the Kendal house. Wow, what a list! Granny Kath's son, my father, was Samuel and my sons' grandfather; a gap of five generations. The relationship was distant enough to be acceptable, near enough to be remarkable. I love the prospect of there being a definite link. My mother was in seventh heaven!

Later on, when Alex and I were exploring the mix of heritage, Alex smiled. 'Mum, you know me and Joanne are together. Well, we might make that permanent. What do you reckon? A double wedding, me an' Az together?'

Well, no argument from me; I've liked Joanne ever since meeting her at least a couple of years ago. So I ask him to phone his dad as soon as poss; might get him before he leaves the shores of Oz.

So… I've been sitting here in the dark, rain drumming on the roof despite the wealth of insulation under the iron and recapping on that birthday event and thinking of Granny travelling to France – if she did. James is back in Darwin; he only stayed overseas for an introductory period – advising and instructing is the terminology, I believe. Usually, men and women of his rank are out of the job at fifty-five so he's already on extra time, or borrowed time as I sometimes fear, but that's just me! The sooner he's home and playing with robots, as I laughingly describe his prime interest, to his irritation, the happier I shall be. A double wedding is something to look forward to! So he'll receive my email and I shall suggest we don't talk widely about the *kindertransport* link, not until we learn more about it, if ever we do. As for links, they don't end there, as the Fletcher thing proves.

I've been delving into the papers in a more organised way and Katherine really has pinned a number together in a sensible sequence. If these make sense, I might scan them all into place and perhaps let her continue to tell the story herself. An unusual but quite attractive way of listening to her own voice, because she does have one!

I poured myself another small whisky – I enjoy it more in the cold, wet weather – and then check the cushion again. Chronological order was James's suggestion so now I must leave 2018 and revert to Katherine's 1932.

Katherine

23

Monday, 18 January 1932

Times are tough, according to Mrs Peach and Mrs Graham.

Mrs Smiles lives up to her name, though; tells me, 'I'm comfy, thanks ter yer uncle.'

She's sleeping in a little store room over the kitchen area and happy to do so, but she gets up very early in the morning, so I'm never late for work nowadays! She still has her house 'up Fellside' but a cousin's living in it at the moment.

Mrs S still pays the rent. Her cousin's come from Newcastle-upon-Tyne, miles north-east from here. She says he was a plater and employed by the shipbuilding but 'That's all gone now 'cause no ships are being sold.'

I had read of the collapse in demand for ships but never thought I'd be in any way touched by it, and I am, just by knowing Mrs S's troubles. Her cousin lost their house, it went with the job, so they're grateful for Mrs S and being able to come here. The local council is going to build lots of houses up near the castle, the idea being to provide jobs as well as cheaper housing eventually, and Mrs S says her cousin's man 'can turn his hand to owt'. I hope so.

Her own son Jack has left to go to Birmingham for a job in the motor industry. and I would have thought a plater would more easily find work building cars. It seems that if you have the money, you want a motor; unemployment, according to the *Gazette*, is actually falling in Birmingham, Coventry and Oxford where the automotive industry is booming. I plan to help her sort out her little room and move some stuff into the box room in the attic. She deserves some comforts.

Mrs Peach has told me that things are a bit more financial at school now; more students are coming every day because more families are being paid unemployment benefits. She thinks it's a good thing to happen but the families are paid according to need. It seems that local officials have been appointed, she says from the town hall, to call and assess the households after a claim is made. They have to ensure folk have no hidden earnings or savings, or other means of support.

Apparently, there's a lot of resentment because some of these officials ask questions that impinge on a family's privacy and, according to Mrs Smiles, 'because they're local they know everyone and in t'pubs later they all gets to know t'other's business'. Seems ghastly and embarrassing.

Because Mrs Smiles was paying the rent on her house that her cousin was now living in, the cousin lost his benefit 'even though he hasn't found a job yet to send her any money to feed littl'uns'. Her paying the rent was considered an undisclosed source of income even though the wife agreed with the landlord who was being paid by Mrs S. How humiliating! The wife and children are still living there but I don't know any other details. Surely the cousin should be rewarded for his efforts to house his family and search for paid work?

Later, after supper. Life suddenly seems so uncertain for me and now I have to think about myself. I know I'm gaining school experience but that's not a qualification in itself. I don't have the money to pay for tuition and I've talked over the whole issue and possibilities and lack of them with Mrs P and the headmaster.

I wonder what Rosie is doing over in Australia, and whether she met up again with JC Williamson and Co. I did write to acknowledge hers I received back in November. I also wrote to her wishing her a very happy Christmas. Here, they have lots of pretty Christmas greeting cards but I couldn't afford one for each person. However, I did find one with lots of snow and a church spire like they have here and sent it to Mum and Dad and marked for all the family. Postage isn't cheap but it's a new idea here and it means you can put everyone on one greeting card and that saves money. I even saw one in Birkett's shop, a birthday card prettily painted, and was tempted to send it to Rosie because she'll be twenty-one on the 25th of this month. But somehow I don't think she'd appreciate it; she's back in the bosom of her father, Uncle George, he who insisted on telling my mum about my baby. My birthday was a month earlier than Rosie's on Christmas Day but I was only eighteen – yet some days I feel much, much older.

Uncle W and Aunt Erica wrote to me for Christmas but they didn't mention my birthday. Actually, we had quite a merry Christmas here. The house seemed to be packed with the boys and their friends. They spent some time next door when Edna was there with her mother, too. They've joined a health and fitness club and also a couple of their friends also go to their school, so they are active, non-stop. I've been taking turns with their laundry too – can't expect Mrs S to run after them too much – and it was sort of suggested it was my due for living here. I have found myself mending their torn clothes quite often, like a proxy mother. And one day, darning a grey sock, I suddenly burst into tears, knowing that, in fact, I am a mother and should have my own little one's socks to mend. Then reason came to the fore…

Saturday, 5 March

Post brought a lovely letter from Uncle W. Pleasant chatty news. He'd watched the 2 February test match in Adelaide and was delighted that Don Bradman was 199 not out and better still, he wrote, Australia beat South Africa by ten wickets. He said there have been horrendous bushfires in Gippsland and men had been trucked over from South Australia to help stop the spread.

He asked how I was managing, repeated his offer to help placate my family in any way he could – he means about my sinning. He made no mention of Rosie. though, and that surprises me. Surely she must be in touch with them? I'm beginning to think she may not have sailed home after all. If she's interstate, in Melbourne with her other grandfather, I'm sure she'd have written me all about it and Uncle W would have known, surely. However, Uncle W and Aunt Erica have settled now in Adelaide. Reading between the lines, he would then, perhaps, have less direct communication with his brother Uncle George and his new wife at Cumquats. That means he may not himself know where Rosie has landed up.

Uncle W did make a couple of less cheery remarks about the Great Depression, as he called it, affecting employment in Adelaide and other cities. I hadn't been able to find out anything about how everyone at home might be affected. After all, it *is* a world situation. Uncle W said he was glad he'd bought their Adelaide house years ago because renters were finding it hard because, when money became tight, landlords simply asked tenants to pay more. He said recent figures indicated almost thirty-two per cent of Australians were out of work and that included teachers and assistants in schools. I would have been in college of course but he did say that Aunt Esther had written from Hahndorf that Dad had to put a man off because of lack of business. That would have affected my teacher training because he would have needed to find my fees. I did surmise from that comment that maybe it was more profitable financially for me to stay here in Kendal. Did it also mean that the business wasn't so busy? Or even losing customers? I could write and ask but would my parents respond to me at all?

Uncle W made one comment I didn't understand. Aussies were angry because a British Bank of England chap had been over there advising what he called a deflationary budget which included cutting many social services. Even worse, this fellow Niemeyer demanded that Australia pay back some loans owed to Britain. That apparently caused a crisis when the premier of New South Wales, Jack Lang, was dismissed from his post because he refused. Uncle W didn't enlarge on that and how he felt about it, which niggled a bit; I'd read nothing of that in the paper here.

I've been a bit slow in noticing – time flies by – but here in England there's widespread unemployment too and it's still causing unhappiness and straitened circumstances at the school.

Mrs Peach says three of her pupils in another class who were over fifteen have been pulled out. She was bitter about it. 'They're girls of course and the first to make sacrifices for the family. Two of them would have been first-class scientists of the Curie brand!'

I had seen something in the *Gazette*, and I read it again after reading Uncle W's letter, that because of Britain's withdrawal from the gold standard and the devaluation of the pound here, interest rates were reduced and that made British exports more competitive than some other countries and that Britain is now heading for a modest economic recovery and a fall in unemployment. But when I mentioned it to Mrs P, she wasn't too optimistic. She said it might be improving in the south, down past London, but it was still bad here in the north-west, particularly in Manchester. For her, that has meant fewer pupils in the past and yet, because young people were the last to be re-employed, ex-pupils were no longer able to make money to help their families. The only saving was their minuscule by comparison tuition fees. (That's Mrs P's phrase.)

24

Monday, 7 March 1932

A letter from Aunt E. It had been posted more than a week after Uncle W's! She was quoting, from a newspaper, I assume – possibly the *Advertiser,* as that's one she used to favour – how people are forced into all sorts of tricks to survive.

'Hundreds if not thousands of fathers have deserted their families to pack a swag and walk around streets and the countryside looking for work. Some have taken to drink. Grown boys sit around, nothing to do, getting into some unsavoury business or another hoping to earn enough pennies to bet on a horse – the racing game keeps going of course – and trying to emulate the bushrangers of the past on the highways, using any clumsy weapon.' She wrote that there were reports of mothers left alone taking in boarders and even cohabiting with those in work so they could earn enough money to put food on the table. Even young girls apparently are being tempted into prostitution.

Oh, journal, I feel sick. I wonder how the Depression might affect Mum and Dad in Hahndorf. How will the church cope? Will the congregations be able to band together to halt the spread of such awful behaviour? My own transgression seems almost mild in comparison yet even as I try to persuade myself, I know the church would be as condemning as ever and my father would always be guided by the pastors' teachings.

However, Aunt E was very understanding of how I might be coping and feeling. I had to wipe my eyes; I miss her so! How I wish I could speak with her over a cup of tea. She made one remark that does puzzle me: asked me if I'd heard from Rosie lately or met up with her. I had been wondering; now I'm sure Rosie did not take ship home. I must try harder to find out.

Wednesday, 9 March

Miracles do happen! A rather grubby envelope was on the doormat as I returned home today and stamped on the back with one of those rubbery things was 'The Noel Coward Theatre, St Martins' Lane, WC' etc. Peeled it on the spot. Only a page of untidy writing but it was from Rosie.

She's been working in something she calls repertory 'down in Portsmouth for most of the winter and now we've just finished a production in London in a play written about Benito Mussolini. Bit dull and political but better paid than rep and the dictator himself wrote it, which did not impress anyone – one review called it an "ego trip". It's horribly boring and actually been taken down after only a few weeks. It left the theatre broke financially and we, the cast, were given our marching orders. By the time this reaches you, I'll be on the train heading for Kendal, so I do hope that will be all right.'

It certainly is! I ran to tell Mrs Smiles.

'It's all right, lass, but it's coming up fer Easter and the boys will be home next week. She'll have to share your room. We'll get it fettled this Sat'day, shall us?'

'Seems she'll be here before then, Mrs S. Good Friday's on the 25th, that right? Don't know if she'll still be staying on.'

'Well, let's have us tea now, lass, an' we'll get sorted soon after.'

'You'll like Rosie, Mrs Smiles.'

'Rosie or Rosalie, lass? I likes ter be correct.'

So I enlarged on a description of my cousin, how she looks and about her always wanting to be a dancer…

I was no sooner helping to clear the tea things when a sharp knock came on the front door and there was Rosie, two soft bags on the steps and they, like her, dripping wet. She came in, looked me up and down, and I held out my arms for a hug. It was a wet one but a friendly one on both sides.

'No brolly, Kath. I left it on the train.'

Mrs S bustled in and took the bags. 'Come wi' me, Rosalie, and I'll show yer where yer can sleep tonight. But first tek off those wet clothes and I'll mek you a cuppa tea, hot an' sugary.'

Her friendly concern lowered Rosie's guard and she seemed to buckle at the knees. I grabbed her and she sobbed all wetly onto my shoulder.

Our ever-efficient Mrs Smiles had Rosie in no time wrapped in an old dressing gown of Uncle W's, and at the kitchen table tucking into a bowl of soup. We heard her story in between mouthfuls. It wasn't all doom and gloom. Apparently, over the Christmas season, the seaside areas along the south coast have a tradition of what Rosie calls musical theatre. The pay wasn't much but the company found her digs and as long as the bed was clean and she could have a warm bath, she was comfy, she said. Someone's name – Paul – kept cropping up, I thought questions could come later.

Saturday, 12 March

First chance this morning to have a good talk with Rosie. She's looking brighter, obviously benefiting from the long sleep she's enjoyed. She was so interested in my work at the school, loved hearing about the students and the work they do. She's curious about Mrs Peach too. To my relief she's happy to have accepted my reason for staying here this extra year; as I explained, it seems beneficial to have some practical experience of a school before going home to enrol at the college in Adelaide. After lunch (dinner, as Mrs Smiles calls it) she insisted on helping Mrs S with a pile of ironing. It's all go with bed sheets and making up the boys' beds, for they'll be here next week in anticipation of Easter. Mrs S helped move Rosie into my room. We pulled the stretcher bed from the little box room into my room. It'll fit.

'Mr Symond's lads tek priority, ladies, as I know tha' knows.'

Rosie has the most amazing plans. 'Katherine, I met up with a couple of lovely ladies. They do music halls and have had a start on the wireless. They don't do plays, don't seem to have scripts, just chat, but they're so funny. Elsie and Doris Waters. One's a posh talker, so they say, and the other like cockney.'

I knew cockney meant an East End accent and that it was on the wireless. Mrs S loved listening to a show put on by Gert and Daisy. I mentioned that show and Rosie laughed.

'That's them, Kath! Lovely women and so friendly. I sang some gay and cheery songs with them one night in the digs and they asked me to come down south with them over the bank holiday – that was in August. They couldn't pay me but said they'd find me digs and pay my meals. All I had to do was entertain with a funny song between their acts. Well, Kath, I was keen – food and digs? Lovely. It was only on for three or four days, then they moved on to Clacton. I was always broke and always hungry. We went to a little theatre in Suffolk, called the Sparrow's Nest – can't remember, was it Lowestoft? The show was called *Gert and Daisy's Party*. That was where I met Paul and he invited me to stay at his flat with some other lads and lassies as he called them. We all slept on the floor and sang the seaside songs and rolled cigarettes and met up each day on the pier and one girl had pinched tins of baked beans from a grocer's stall and we opened them with a screwdriver and ate them cold. The boys bought us beers and perry if we…well, if we did as they wanted.'

At this point I went to the kitchen and made a pot of tea. I was shocked, I think, but who was I to preach? I had to be matter of fact. Rosie was broke… And that must have happened last year, so what has she done since then, over the winter for instance? I thought she would tell me eventually. When I took our cups back to the room, she was just sitting, deep in thought.

'Kath, I met up with some lovely young cricketing lads who were friends of Paul. All hopeful of one day playing for their country, all in some sort of senior college. Don't know how they can afford it but they all seemed to get allowances from their families and they follow the cricket teams all over the country to watch and shout support. Not sure if that isn't a kind of madness. Anyway, they have all kinds of connections and one of them suggested I sail home in September with them on the *Orontes*…'

'Goodness gracious, Rosie! That's a huge cost! You must have made a lot of money on your am drams!'

'Katherine, you know very well I'm beyond amateur dramatics. Do stop teasing. As a matter of fact, I wanted to talk to you about the scheme I have in case you're still interested in going back to enrol to be a teacher in Adelaide.'

Well, I can't remember how she explained it but she can apply to be on an entertainment crew on the ship. She says they have them on most ships. We didn't have one coming over of course because that was a modified freight trip. Rosie would be paid not very much but would have her passage, and that includes a bunk in a shared cabin and all meals. The cricketing boys are already booked; they worked that as soon as it was known the English cricket team would be on board for the Ashes.

This Paul she mentioned seems to be of a better sort than she'd led me to believe. Though it seems they all wanted the same home comforts, journal. Paul said he could fix it – the concert party trip. For her on her own of course; and I don't think I can sing and dance. I didn't tell Rosie I'm unhappy about trying to go back to Hahndorf and home. Nor did I mention why. In fact, I'm really enjoying working at the school and living here in comfort and helping Mrs S when the boys come for the hols. I think I'll tell her to make her own plans.

Next day, Sunday

A lovely springtime morning. I cajoled Rosie to come for a walk and maybe a stop to buy a pie for a lunch to eat and do some real walking. I thought long about her last night, journal; didn't sleep much. Everyone else but her knows of my baby, little Avril. I shall tell her; I know she won't tell the boys when they come here for half-term.

I told her. Matter of factly, no embellishments. She stopped still. We were near the pie shop.

She was on the point of taking a bite before we reached the garden seat but just stood there with her mouth open. 'No. *No!*' she shouted at me. 'Kath, how…why…when?'

And there in the street I burst into tears and I couldn't stop.

She took my arm and we found the wooden seat. 'Now, Kath. Tell me everything. I promise you I will not in any way censure you.'

And she sat, the uneaten pies on her lap between us, her arm around my shoulder, as I recounted it all: Kris, Ralph's belief in him as a friend; Mum's anger and hurt; Dad's saying for me to never come home would be too soon; then Uncle W's kindness and help…everything. It grew cold and I was drained, oblivious to the drizzle as it started to wet us and everything around us.

Then she stood up. 'Come on, cuz. And I promise, I'll not say anything to anyone. This is a hard world and we've both struck out on our own and done something very different to what was expected of us. Let's go home, make a pot of tea and enjoy some peace before our noisy boy cousins burst the bubble.'

Funny language, but we did just that.

Very late in the evening, I'm sitting on the edge of my bed and Rosie's asleep in the other one, actually snoring! I'm writing this in pencil so I don't spill ink on the sheets. It was so good having Rosie to talk to and she said it was comforting for her. She unburdened herself to me and I feel shocked, which is almost hypocritical of me because look what I've done – sinned and told lies over months. I am so conscious of the state I'd been in at this time last year. My darling little Avril was born on the 25th. It's almost her first birthday, had she lived. I can't cry, though; that grief is deep within me.

I'm too aware that Rosie has been in awful digs while touring with the playhouse people and was so broke at one time after those two ladies befriended her, that she had nothing except glasses of water for two days and nights. Then Paul took pity on her; he bought her fish and chips – she said it was 'cod an' two pennorth' and blissful. She was so grateful, she slept with him and he gave her a whole pound. They did it again a few times then, when he went to another town for another show and she wasn't given a part, she slept with someone called Ian and he gave her a job as an usher in a cinema.

She said it was less hard to do it as time went on. Altogether over nearly three months she slept with eleven men and just before she sent me the letter, she'd been in a hospital recovering from a miscarriage! It happened in her digs and she became infected and now she's been told she may never be able to have another baby. Oh, journal!

Yet we are now both safe here in Uncle W's Beastbanks house. We agreed it was time to count our blessings and do some serious thinking. We've shared secrets, journal. Rosie's isn't known like mine is by everyone, but I won't tell on her.

Oh, I'm so tired. Goodnight, journal.

Sally

25

Sunday, 7 October 2018

It's been a miserable winter this year. Rain, rain and more of the stuff. They say this winter is Adelaide's wettest since…oh, ages. I know it's good for the garden, setting up a bank of moisture in the soil before summer, but it's not good for my morale. Last time I read Katherine's papers, it was raining and that was more than three months ago; winter's now behind us, theoretically. Today is Sunday 7 October and I'm here in spring, heading for summer – not that the weather is any indication. Usually here in Adelaide it's the long weekend for Labour Day and the kids go back to school soon for the last term all dressed in summer gear. Not so this year, I bet – today's forecast is only seventeen degrees.

It's been a frustrating couple of months altogether; unresolved issues. My mother came a number of times reporting on her redecorating; she moved on to the living room from the bathroom and kitchen. I went around to see the results and it was most attractive, very different, I think, to what had obviously been Dad's taste – and why not?

Then she brought around some material for a window curtain, upset because her eyesight couldn't allow her to sew a straight seam corresponding to the pattern, so of course I offered to do that for her. She *is* my mother! One thing led to another and she commandeered my boys into some odd jobs at weekends. They enjoyed doing that and then I had to listen to how Nan Emily enjoyed chatting with Ari and Jo, as it seems their fiancées prefer to be called. Don't mistake me, I'm thrilled the four young people are so friendly and their Nan likes them. So do I and so does James, and to have my mother's approval is apparently the ultimate accolade in their eyes. Great. Terrific. But do we need to hold post-mortems on every aspect of each relationship every mealtime? It's all so time-consuming. I so miss my sensible James.

After his initial enthusiasm about the *kindertransport* connection, I found little more about the topic. James's friend's wife translated the French note and in fact it was written by a German in tentative French requesting help for a young lad called Pieter in Holland who had come from Germany with his family to make his way to England. Strangely, there were thanks to be given to Mrs Downham for the potatoes. Potatoes? *Pommes de terre*, she writes. Does that mean humble spuds? She lost me; can't fathom this one out.

Writers of fiction are suspected of being a little odd, as we deal in imagination and untruths (so I've had it said to me). Similarly, police officers, medicos of all levels of expertise, are also dedicated to their tasks, their duties, but are as entitled to a separate life away from their chosen professions as I do. Also, when they do revert to being who they are and not what, they can be criticised as if they're unhuman. We're all who; the what is secondary. I know that conversely I've complained about people interrupting my writing when I'm onto a good thing, but there are also times when I need to stop and think and forget about a topic because life, real life, contemporary life, intervenes.

Okay, homily ended. However, I haven't totally neglected Katherine. I've been enthusiastically researching all her papers, and the ones from the chair cushion padding particularly. I'm interested in all this earlier theatrical stuff so I tackled the State Library about the possibility of southern English amateur dramatic companies having links with the JC Williamson group. I confirmed Rosalie's earlier comment about the Taits taking over the firm back in 1931 and that led me into an absorbing few weeks reading up on the company. Started by James Cassius Williamson in America – that explains the JayCee acronym – they built fine theatres in all states in the Commonwealth and New Zealand. Though their main interest was in presenting legitimate theatrical productions, the firm was one of the pioneers of the film industry in Australia and involved also in radio and television. I had not realised that our – James and mine – favourite Adelaide theatre, Her Majesty's, was one of their group. I knew it had been built on the site of the Tivoli, because the Tiv has been mentioned by my mother a number of times, but I don't know how often she went there. Her lifestyle as a younger woman was quite limited.

While looking up all these old shows, I was reminded of Dad telling me how, before they were married, he took her to the final show at the Tiv and it was a comedy, *The Sentimental Bloke*. Dad loved Aussie humour. Less to his personal taste was the last attraction at the old Theatre Royal, then in Hindley Street, shortly after they were married and before the theatre was demolished. It was the Bolshoi Ballet and he said Mum was entranced. After that, the JC Williamson group reopened the refurbished Tivoli as Her Majesty's.

All this theatrical stuff I found fascinating. Then it occurs to me I can't remember Mum ever speaking of the ballet. She may have done – she often then, and still, accuses me of never listening! So I pick up the phone.

'Hello, Mum it's me…'

'Hello, you. I'm just having a cuppa. Good timing.'

'I've dug out some info on the Tivoli. Seem to remember, didn't you and Dad attend the last show there, Aussie comedy monologue or something of the kind?'

'Wow! Long time since… Yes, I think so… I think it was that C.J. Dennis poetry story. I don't think I enjoyed it – well, not as much as your dad did.' Her memory's ticking over now, I can practically hear it clicking. 'We didn't go very often – his work, you know – but I do remember the ballet he took me to at the old Royal, the Bolshoi. I was blown away – it was beautiful. I'm glad you rang, dear. I want to ask you…'

I excused myself after a bit of miscellaneous chit-chat. Felt a bit guilty, actually; she was obviously in the mood, but I can bring up the topic again sometime.

Rosalie is the reason I'd started delving into the theatrical and drama events, looking for links. How was she involved in theatre and with whom and for how long? Was she going to take ship? Would Katherine shed her family worries and go with her? Could she if she wanted to?

I'm desperate to find something in Katherine's notes about her activities just before the 1939 war. That little tin of souvenirs, if that's the word, is so tantalising. It's becoming harder and harder to imagine my Granny Kath undergoing such mental and moral turmoil as must have been involved if she undertook any task resembling espionage; she of the silver-gold-grey chignon, laughing blue-grey eyes and lavender-coloured cardigans encasing, supposedly, that strong moral compass. Inking her thumbprint, picking locks… It would have been sorely tested enough by knowing of Rosalie's behaviour and her measuring it against her own sin.

I'm surprised this account was not hidden in the depths of that big cushion, cleverly disguised like everything else within its buttoned and zippered wrapping. Surely she would have wanted that little tin to burn, too, to be thrown out with the old basket-weave chairs and destroyed before discovery. Okay, it was Rosalie sleeping around but Katherine, the so very proper Granny Kath I knew, condoned her behaviour. The family has a flaw; why don't I feel triumphant? Because I'm not my mother. Oops.

It's time to sort out my thinking and there's no place better than my garden. While rather brutally lopping at the roses in the garden today for a second flowering – I hope they'll survive – I found myself wondering how much of this Rosalie story I can tell my mum. She has been so keen for me to find the truth about Granny Kath. The more I think of it, the more I think she's secretly hoping to find flaws in her pseudo-mum and thus recoup some of her own lost self-esteem? So I cannot mention any connection with Germany – yet. Imagine what she would make of that.

One reason I feel I'm jumping around in my research, not focusing, is fair enough: I too have a life here. Now my two daughters-in-lawto-be have discovered they share a birthday, 18 January, and want to have that as their joint wedding! Okay, but that's a Friday, so I hope to persuade them to have the ceremony on the Saturday. However, the girls will decide and custom declares I can relax as it's their parents' privilege to allow their parents to organise their wishes. Woohoo!

Another of my difficulties in knotting this story together stems,somewhat obscurely, from my preoccupation in analysing the success of my own marriage, something I've seldom bothered about. Seems okay to me. However, it came about because of a chat in the garden when the boys were helping me, one doing some overdue pruning and the other mowing the lawn. I poured a beer and the questions followed but not about the wedding; happily they both accept that the wedding, however elaborate the planning, is but the gateway to marriage, and that it's marriage that matters. That led to their theorising about James and me, having been happily married for so long (their phrase).

Made me see myself as the boys see me. Aaron ventured his opinion that we were contented as a couple because we had so many reunions after James returned from various detachments. Alex said that it was more to the point that we each had time away from each other. Knowing their dad was thirty when we married, they wondered if they were too young. So we discussed that aspect at length and it prompted my own consequent self-analysis.

I realise even contentment needs questions at times; nevertheless, it has all broken into my Katherine-concentration-time to put away the secateurs, go back indoors and settle to some more of her note taking. They're so well put together in this collection, she's telling her tale herself. And I am so enjoying listening and learning!

Katherine

26

Saturday, 17 September 1932

Yesterday I saw Rosie off on the train to London; at least she's familiar with the route. The last few days have been chaotic with packing and choosing new dresses and mending old but useful ones that had arrived here in boxes after her return. She actually noted down what accessories she needed for various characterisations and we spent one merry day seeking out a feather boa – apparently a long scarf-like thing to fling dramatically around one's shoulders when performing. When we arrived home that day, she put on an impromptu song and dance act in the living room. Nick and Stevie howled with laughter. Being still school holidays, young Edna had come in from next door – like the boys, she's a regular table-jigsaw fiend – and she giggled quite uncontrollably, setting us all into tears of laughter again.

When Rosie put on the phonogram and played one of the scenes from the *Mikado* with such elaborate and inspired typical gestures, even Mrs Smiles chortled in her cup of tea. That inspired Mrs S. She disappeared and returned about a quarter hour later with a vividly, exquisitely decorated Chinese fan. From the attic of all places. Rosie embraced her and hooted in delight, so we had an encore!

Well, with these theatrical props – so out of this world – we all recognised the talent we'd been cossetting behind the sober front doors of Beastbanks. Mrs Smiles lived up to her name and when Rosie mimicked her older friends Gert and Daisy, Mrs Smiles even snorted with laughter. That set us all off again. Mrs S and I helped Rosalie press, stitch and sometimes adjust the fitting of some of the stage outfits, performance units as Rosalie referred to them. Most dresses were rather elaborate, some quite risqué but none too revealing – even allowing for modern trends. She claimed she'll be the only junior member of the concert party on the *Orontes* but was quite unworried.

'It's a means of travelling home, Kath. The ship calls at Gibraltar and Naples, and Paul will take me to see the ruins of Pompeii under Vesuvius. Then on 8 October we have a day in Kandy at Ceylon and on the 18th we dock in Fremantle. Oh, I'll feel like home then, I think. Already I've moved around this country a bit, seen a few things, done many I don't want ever to repeat.' At that, she gave a sad little moue. 'My papa will be pleased to see me. I'll not tell him the whole story and I know you'll be discreet. I'll play things very carefully by ear, Kath. And that goes for you – and the baby and all that. Whatever else they don't need to know, they won't learn from me. I promise. I'm not sure if the ship goes to Adelaide after Fremantle, or Melbourne. If it's Adelaide, I plan to visit uncle William in Adelaide and if it's Melbourne I'll see my Gran'pa Smythe for a while then take the train to Renmark. I want to meet this new stepmother of mine…I think!'

She grinned. 'I'm so happy these months are over, really I am. It has been an experience and if I've proved anything, it's that home is best, even picking cumquats, but only for a while. I'll write to you and let you know.'

The day came. A last hug and she was gone. Her theatrical aspirations had not been met but at least she had made the effort and come through it all. Her scars are well hidden. I only hope she will write to me. I sat down to do some darning on the boys' socks and, only briefly, pondered on what I might have done on the ship had I accompanied her. Time was going by and I had to bite the bullet, as Uncle W once said to me.

I later decided I should take my own advice and write to my mother. Hard to know if she reads what I send. I hadn't written her for her birthday at the start of the month this year. Not after her last letter to me. With Rosie here, even though the school was closed for the holidays, I hadn't put pen to paper. I looked at the birthday card I'd bought – these little message tokens are mass-produced now. All they require is the briefest of messages when words are hard to find. I'll give a brief apology for lateness and send it off tomorrow. Better than nothing. Perhaps.

Sunday, 30 October

Oh, this Depression! Schools are being affected by lack of funding. Mrs Peach has been told to make economies and I'm possibly going to be one of them! For the moment, she has made a case with the governors to keep me because apparently I'm very useful with the older students. It may be different next year but I know I do seem to find topics of interest to them. I can't stray from the curriculum but I can talk about different aspects of a place or an event, or even give them ideas for filling their time at home.

The young plants from Mrs Graham and the little vegetable gardens seem to be a great success. Those who started one a season or two seasons ago are benefiting and even if the carrots are an odd shape they are quite edible and the race to grow the longest carrot is apparently one of the competitions. Cabbages grow incredibly well here. One young lad planted a stone from a peach and it actually shot to a plant and because it's against a south-facing wall, one day – if he's patient enough – it may bear fruit! It's an achievement anyway. I showed some of the lads how radishes, that grow so quickly, can be put in the oven with a scrag end of lamb, half an hour before the lamb is cooked, and they're like baby turnips but more tender. That idea has caught on with their mums – they're all growing radishes.

At the start of this year, I paid a shilling for three large bags of horse manure. Mr Peach the postman met a man on his rounds who would cart them to the school playground. This achieved, we placed the bags in a sunny spot where once a hole had been sunk for whatever reason I know not! The playground was on quite a slope and at the lower end rain collected that was swept sideways into a drain by the wall. Not a bad site for a garden. We emptied the horse manure in the pit then four of the older boys were asked to fill a wheelbarrow or a cart with soil from the edge of the common on the overgrown road side of the fence, and bring the soil here. Mrs Graham had given me a dozen seed potatoes and the headmaster, after school one afternoon, carefully placed each one into the tatty pit, as it was already named. Each tatty was marked by a stick. For reasons of diplomacy, we thought it best no one student could lay claim to their potato and its produce.

The potatoes this first year had yielded a remarkable bounty. Our first harvest was in June before the holidays. Mr Sutton supervised the digging up of three seed potatoes and it was agreed the potatoes were delicious but still small and the youngest children would each have one. Three seed potatoes yielded enough for one new potato for each child in the youngest two classes, and one for each of their teachers. We then agreed to wait for another two weeks and then the next three seed potatoes would be dug up, for children with bigger stomachs, as Mrs Peach put it.

A week later

The potatoes had grown – exponentially – and we all thought it a most rewarding exercise. The little students had already whetted the bigger ones' appetites with tales of their special spuds. With only one more week to go before the school broke up for the holidays, it was agreed the final dig, for the students with the biggest stomachs, would be on the following Wednesday, last day of term. Yet Fate intervened.

We adults had all heard of the riots in Bristol. Mrs S was positively loquacious about the government. We knew of the hunger marches; unemployment was nearly three million nationally and the National Unemployed Workers Movement had organised hunger marches from different areas, protesting against the means test of 1932. They were scheduled to meet up in London at Hyde Park. A petition was organised with a million-plus signatures demanding the abolition of the test. The first contingent of marchers left from Glasgow on 26 September, they had the longest march, and it was planned they'd all gather with others on 27 October in Hyde Park. I heard from Mrs Smiles that many from Kendal were joining a northern contingent at Preston.

The marchers had not received much in the way of publicity on their way to London but, having reached the capital, I read in the paper that '…they met an almost blanket condemnation as a threat to public order, verging upon the hysterical in the case of some of the more conservative press'. The government confiscated the petition and police used batons and all kinds of force to subdue the marchers. The Metropolitan Police Commissioner, a Lord Trenchard, mobilised a force of 70,000 police, so I read. Serious violence erupted in and around the park, with mounted police being used to break up the formations of demonstrators; across central London seventy-five people had to be hospitalised. Because the NUWM was a Communist movement, the home secretary, Sir John Gilmour, was questioned in the House of Commons as to whether the marches were being funded by Moscow. Panic in the heights of government.

This was all distressing enough but what really cut home to us schoolies was our home turf. Our last harvest of potatoes, planned for the last days of term, had been raided!

Our project had been well publicised by the eagerness and enthusiasm of the children. The theft of the potatoes, the special spuds, prompted a huge outcry. It had all been planned: the local newspaper was to come and witness our last dig, the whole project having aroused great interest in other schools, Now, on this last dig, there were few precious potatoes left to harvest. Most had been taken. Luckily, the remainder were big ones and just enough when cut in half for each of the big stomachs to have a half. Our students learned many lessons of life that day, not all of them favourable.

However, on the last day of term, a farmer's cart pulled up and a Mr Fletcher donated to every single child in the school a big fresh potato ready for cooking. To the school he donated twenty seed potatoes ready for next year. He said he admired the initiative and would always help out with any school garden project. It gave a warm feeling that offset the other disappointment.

27

Saturday, 5 November 1932

I've learned the history of Guy Fawkes and now I know that burning
the guy on this date is a national celebration. I remember how last year
I was so miserable at this time. The students from school have built an
enormous bonfire – well, more accurately, they've contributed to the
community fire. If it's a pleasant evening, I shall go along to it.

More to the point, the headmaster called me in today and told
me they can't afford to pay for my position after this year. So I have
until Friday 16 December at the school. After that, what? Mrs Peach
suggested today I may be able to volunteer through the council to help
with disadvantaged children. I know I don't have to pay rent but I do
have costs to meet and need some kind of wage. What can I do? I'm
regretting I didn't go back to Australia when I had the chance.

Friday, 25 November

I've had an unhappy month. Nothing from my mother after her birthday
card; nothing from Rosie about her trip over what was presumably a
safe arrival – somewhere. The more I think, the more I'm convinced I
should have gone. Even with the cost of shipping, I could pay, but all
this suspicion about Hitler in Germany is limiting the availability of
ships. Obviously, I haven't read enough about the man's rise into power.
Besides which, I'm sure I did read a while ago that his political party,
called the Nazis, suffered an unexpected loss to the nationalists. Here
in Britain there was so much economic depression and it seemed to me
people were confused between communism and fascism. Surely Moseley
was giving the downtrodden workers some hope?

I read constantly about Moseley allying himself to the ideals of the

Hitler Nazis in Germany. I wonder how all the news is being received at home, in Hahndorf? During the Great War, people had been made to feel like traitors. On the face of it, it seemed to me that his ideas of order were constructive, then, unexpectedly one day in a different newspaper, I read of his dislike for Jews. I fail to understand his logic. It goes way beyond simple dislike. *The Times* reported how in Berlin they've burned books written by Jews and opponents of Nazism – public fires. Horrible!

I remember Julie Todmann, Mum's friend in Hahndorf. Her son Michael works for Dad and he's older than me; used to look after me if I went into the workshop area. They were Jewish, my family was Lutheran and a dirty word at that time. More so than being Jewish. Prejudice is capricious.

Thursday, 8 December

Read in the paper that England won the first test in Sydney. By now, then, Rosie should be somewhere she wanted to be. Surely I should be receiving a letter soon. Also I read that this Hitler in Germany declares all Germans are members of his Nazi party. Huh?

I'm in a quandary about what to do in January when there'll be no school classroom work for me. I must make plans. But first there's Christmas. I'm a little surprised that Uncle W's boys don't seem to miss their mother and father, and little Alicia, at such a time as Christmas. Uncle W and Aunt E have written them for Christmas and they prattled on about some of the things happening at home. I'm missing my family rather terribly, more so than I thought possibly after their harsh words. I guess it's all about knowing one's place in the world. Who said that?

Friday, 6 January 1933

It's Epiphany. Well, I've had my birthday. After the next Christmas, I'll become of age, twenty-one. What does it really mean to me? Not much. It was a happy Christmas but only Mrs Smiles remembered it was my birthday too. No letters from home, not even from Rosie. I suppose they feel I've really cut my ties; ties they no longer consider binding – obviously.

There's no work in this town for females. I'm quite at a loss. Uncle W's boys are back at school now and, I suspect, glad to be. They grumbled at times that their Christmas was too quiet. Many of their friends were elsewhere for their Christmases; with relatives, I guess, as is traditional. It's only me and Mrs S. Mrs Graham next door is rather concerned for her sister, my Mrs Peach from school. Apparently she's unwell. I'm not sure with what – I have a suspicion it may be something rather nasty. Mrs G is all doom and gloom.

Later that evening

Edna has just been around to return a book she borrowed. I asked her about her mother and she told me her father has confided in her that it's thought to be cancer. She's soon to have a radiography test which should show the cause. I shall be so sorry if Mrs P is as sick as they seem to think. Then I wonder, what about her work? Surely she'll need me more than ever?

Meanwhile, Mrs Smiles has asked my advice about all the jams in the cellar. There are jars and jars and, what's more, some wine bottles thick with dust. We've set ourselves to some logical arranging of them all and also to checking the age of the wines. I resolved that after they're all sorted out, I'll write to Uncle W to determine his wishes about this stuff; also Aunt Erica's views on the jams. So for now I have employment of a kind; it's unpaid, obviously, but I have lodgings and I shall have to watch my savings for the board part of the board and lodging equation.

Tuesday, 24 January

I've just read about an unpleasant controversy in Adelaide at the third test match. They're calling it the bodyline match. Douglas Jardine, the English captain, apparently told his bowlers to hate the Australians, all because of the massive run-scoring by Don Bradman. The paper seems to be saying Jardine wants his team to play dirty. He's alleged to have instructed his fast bowlers, Larwood and Voce, to bowl on the line of the batsman's legs and body and restrict their stroke-playing options with cordons of leg-side fielders. The Australian captain, Bill Woodfull, it's said, stated that 'there are two teams on the field but only one is playing cricket'. Apparently the feeling is so strong, the MCC here in England has agreed to bring its players home should the Australian board decide to cancel the tour. Oh, I feel that's shocking on the part of the England team. Quite embarrassing. I'm glad Stevie and Nick are back at school or sparks would have flown.

A letter has arrived from an address in Suffolk, quite a surprise, and addressed to Rosie. Mrs S suggested I deal with it. To send it to Australia when I'm not sure if she's in Melbourne or Renmark would be wasteful of time and effort. I opened it. The sender was a David Downham. Apparently he's a cricket man. No mention of the bodyline controversy, of course. He writes that he hopes Rosalie doesn't mind him writing but she'd left this contact address behind at their digs. I don't remember Rosie talking about a David.

Reading further, seems to me he's more a flyer type than a cricket man – he's been taking lessons on something called a Rapide. Said that he's been reading about that flyer, Bert Hinkler, an Australian, having 'met with misfortune' while attempting to fly in record time from London to Darwin. Continues, implying it was a bit foolish to attempt the flight in a Puss Moth. Apparently, Hinkler's body hasn't yet been found. I hadn't heard anything of this. I think him a brave adventurer, that Bert, whereas this David sounds rather a playboy type, such as my so proper brother Ralph would call fast. I put the letter in my room; eventually I'll respond and tell him Rosie's in Australia.

Mrs S and I had been celebrating our completion of the jam sorting from the cellar over a pot of tea when young Edna arrived. Her mother – my Mrs P – is to go into hospital for that radiology and tests then to recuperate. The school would like me to help out their new temporary teacher for the rest of this term. If so, I'm to report tomorrow. Oh, relief! Sorry for Mrs P, but at least she's embarking on a cure and I do need the money and the enjoyment. I love the work.

26 January

Adolf Hitler, the flamboyant leader of the Nazi Party in Germany has outplayed President von Hindenberg of Germany to become chancellor. Apparently, the country had been on the brink of civil war, with Hitler's National Socialists and the Communists constantly waging bloody street battles. This Hitler is not popular in his country; many see him as a rabble rouser, a Johnny-come-lately who dropped out of school, was a house painter and latterly an army corporal. The paper goes on to say Hitlerism was born out of the middle classes' longing for order, bankers' fear of Bolshevism, and industrialists' and the militaristic Junkers' nostalgia for German *Machtpolitik*. I thought a lot about the Todmans back home as I read more of Hitler's attitude to the Jewish people.

Wednesday, 1 March

Now the Reichstag building in Berlin has gone up in flames and the Communists are blamed. The newspaper reports say Hitler has obtained a decree suspending all legal guarantees of personal liberty, of freedom of speech and the press and the right of assembly; Herr Hitler is now the dictator.

There's also an article bemoaning the recent Ashes series as the 'most acrimonious series yet played'. I seem to recall Uncle W saying, when something fell below his standards, it's not cricket. Cricket to him was the apogee of gentlemanly sport. Bet he thinks differently now.

I wonder how he is, and Aunt Erica. How I wish I could more easily contact them, or that they'd even answer my long ago letters! They do write to the boys at school – Stevie told me some news over Christmas – so that's something.

Now I'm reminded of that one for Rosie from David Downham. If his address is current, I'll let him know about Rosie being in Australia. Only polite, I suppose.

I must now turn my thinking to the tatty pit in the school grounds – more potatoes! The headmaster told me some pleasing news: some families are contriving canny ways of planting spuds in old baskets and moving them around the garden to catch every bit of sunlight. Two students have reported that their mothers, good friends, are growing cabbage plants in old laundry baskets. Some of these houses have only about six feet of cobbled walkway out the back to a primitive toilet, nearly always in shadow and wet from frequent scrubbing. Planting potatoes in such conditions truly is enterprising, but enterprising these people are. A Mrs Cox has planted cabbages in an old trug, very shallow soil, and has put the trug atop their toilet at the bottom of the garden to catch the sun. Cabbages are shallow-rooting; no good for carrots, though. Well done!

Saturday, 25 March

Two years since my little Avril was born. I see little toddlers of that age playing in the puddles outside, dressed in rubber welly boots; wet, dirty and happy as can be. I wish, and wonder…

I read that the Nazis have opened their first concentration camp at Dachau, near Munich. Rumours are rife that they're to imprison the Jews. It seems that no longer can they buy kosher meat in Germany and that Jews are fleeing the country as quickly as they can, some leaving behind their homes, furnishings and treasured possessions intact, in order to escape. Many are coming to England. I wondered yet again about the Todmans in Hahndorf. Julie has been Mum's special friend for years now. The thought of such persecution sickens me. Yet the German air minister Hermann Goering is reported as assuring the world that Germany's Jews are not in danger. Lies!

Heard late morning that Mrs Peach is resting at home after her treatment. The wonders of science and Madame Curie. Mrs Graham popped her head over the hedge to let me know. Also, Edna's no longer at school; she'll look after her mother at home. I knew Mrs P had left the hospital. The headmaster visited her and his wife took a bunch of flowers. Mr S told all the staff that she hopes to be back next term and that I'll stay on for another term if I'm willing. (Which of course I am!) One of the teachers in the junior classes will take on the teaching role and I'll work more with the littlies, as I can do things with them unsupervised, said the head. Mrs P did say she'd rather not have visitors until she feels a little stronger.

I'm busy making myself a new dark skirt for school. Four inches below the knee is the fashion and it also saves fabric...

28

Later that evening, Saturday, 25 March 1933

A strange happening this afternoon. A very loud knock on the door and Mrs S came up to the box room where we've now put the Singer sewing machine.

'It's for you, miss – that David Downham as sent the letter.'

Well, this was unexpected after I wrote that he'd missed Rosie. A quick check of my hair in the mirror and I walked downstairs. He was waiting in the hall, a tall fellow in a leather jacket, holding his hat, some goggles and long driving gloves in his one free hand. He put out the other one and we shook hands. I like that approach.

'I hope it's not inconvenient to call, Miss Flack.'

I shook my head and smiled. 'Not at all. Call me Katherine. You obviously received my letter. Come into the living room.'

He's very pleasant-looking; eyes wide apart, as my mother would say. His loosely brushed black hair fell over his forehead as he spoke and there and then, in that first moment, I wanted to stroke it back into place! Those eyes were smiling as intently as his generous mouth. I offered to take his jacket and hung it over the back of a spare chair. I grinned inwardly as Mrs S brought in a pot of tea and some scones, noticing her eyes flick up and down and over.

'I'm sorry to have missed Rosie. She was – still is, I'm sure – a beautiful singer. She was great fun to be with.'

'Are you in the show business, Mr Downham?'

He smiled even more widely. 'Please call me David. No. I'm a sports teacher at a boys' school. Love cricket, that's how I…well…'

'Yes, Rosie told me about her cricketing friends and indeed it was one of them who encouraged her on this trip back to Australia.'

'Yes, Paul. Nice fellow. He'll look after her. Are you into the show business, Katherine?'

I told him not so much as I don't have the time. I agreed I missed my Australian family; hoped to return soon; meanwhile, I wanted to see something of my great-great-grandmother Beatrice's home country.

He spoke of his learning to fly, but having to give it up; lessons cost too much. If war breaks, though, he intends to enlist for aircrew. We discussed if and when war might arrive. He thought Hitler abhorrent and feared for Portsmouth, a vital harbour and his home town.

'Oh, you're not from Lowestoft then?'

'I've been staying there for work – you'll know of the unemployment of course? It's a good school and though I would rather be nearer my family home, I'm fortunate to have the position. I met Paul and the other cricketing fellows because they were allowed a few hits on the school grounds at weekends, under my supervision. Some of them actually are old boys.'

Ahah! He spoke of his family – they all seem to be in teaching or something related to education. His mother loves to cook and bake and his father loves to eat it all! I laughed and I talked of my Hahndorf in-laws and how my Grandma Flach loved to bake *pfefferkuchen* and I made them sometimes, especially for the boys when they were home. We put the economy to rights over that pot of tea and he asked if he might call again or, if he can't take the time off to drive all this way, might he telephone me.

Of course I said yes, journal. He gave me a card with his school's address and also one with his home address. He recommended I try his Pompey address during the long school breaks and that's when I learned that Pompey was Portsmouth! In term time, the Lowestoft school would give him any telephone message. As he stood, he asked if I'd ever ridden on a motorbike. I admitted I hadn't but loved the freedom they seem to suggest. He laughed at that and said perhaps one summer day I might like to give it a try.

I helped him with his jacket and at the door he shook hands again then donned his cap, goggle and gloves. What a deep-throated roar that bike made as he moved off up the hill. He's staying with some family friends in Bowness, not far to go, and then tomorrow he's setting off early to return to his school in time to do some prep. He has some kind of sports day on the Monday to supervise and also helps with algebra because he enjoys it and the other teacher said he infects the boys with his enthusiasm – not a bad thing with algebra.

I like him. I hope he gets in touch again and, if so, well, I am a modern woman!

Sally

29

Tuesday, 6 November 2018

So detailed, so colourful and so lengthy. I really enjoyed reading about her meeting with David. After all, I can guess the outcome – I already know him to be my dad's dad! And Katherine writes so easily – it follows fluently, situation after situation. I'm wondering how to fit them in book form. I'm most reluctant to fill the gaps, create links, with some inventive fiction. Should I make her fluid journal entries into a Part Two within the covers? I could simply interweave them with my summations as I've done so far. Who can advise? I'll ask James as a first stop – he has a good eye and ear.

Firstly, I now know of the potato connection. Reader, you may remember the French translation given on a tiny note in the dental powder tin. Is that Pieter the Pieter of the Ostermann family? Hard to determine the times. Goodness, this woman jumps about!

Now James…he's home at the moment on eleven weeks sick leave. R&R. Sounds an odd length of time but he'll need it all. Poor bloke has a crushed knee, something to do with fitting a wheel on an aircraft. Routine job, says my husband, never mind the details. He's embarrassed, annoyed and in pain. I'm really sorry for him. He can't walk and the pain is obviously severe. He's had surgery – looks a most unfriendly wound.

I'll be driving him to rehab a number of times in the coming weeks and I don't mind at all. For myself, I'm glad to have him at home and to know he won't be going away again. He's done his bit, as Alex and Aaron assure me, and there's always a grain of worry at the back of my mind when he's away and, there's no denying it, incidents are fairly commonplace. I can't help thanking my lucky stars that he'll be here too for his boys' weddings in January. By then, he should be walking comfortably enough to enjoy the occasion. I hope. Right now, patience is called for and James never was one for waiting around.

Back to the book. He wants to know how it's coming along. I've given him the draft to date and he listened eagerly to my recorded episodes. He's intrigued at this first real introduction of David Downham, his grandfather. He'll check some of Katherine's notes about the British RAF for me. He's well-read and knows a lot of Service history and facts. Terrific!

However, his treatments are far more important than any possible story. Too soon, it's Christmas and then the weddings. He always likes having a project so I may hand over some more of those chair cushion papers to peruse as he recovers – I know he'll check and double check. Knowing that, I don't feel too guilty about my own neglect of it.

He thinks that when Gran and I had that chat on what would have been her David's hundredth birthday, she had her facts wrong about his enlistment in the RAF. He maintains that had David been a boy apprentice, perhaps he would have been taken on in 1934/35 as a trainee. However, says James, grown men of twenty-three or thereabouts needed to wait until enlistment. I shall leave him to check that for me – Gran, though as bright as a button, may have made an error.

He's so ready to investigate further the possible connection between Katherine and the *kindertransport*, yet even he's wondering where to start and if there would be implications. As she's dead, bless her, it's unlikely there will be any complications – other than complimentary, that is. To be quite truthful, I'm unsure what ominous secrets about Granny Kath I'm likely to find.

James does like my approach to Katherine's stories. He doesn't mind the date-hopping, if it's clearly indicated who is when.

'One thing, Sal: have you told Mum yet about baby Avril?'

'No, I couldn't find the words. I still think it'll be best to let her read the finished story and then I can frame the event properly, in context, using Gran's own words. And now there's this refugee project to complicate matters.'

'Yep, I think that's best, Sal, really do. It'll come as a shock just blurted out...'

'James! I wouldn't blurt.'

'Okay, luv, but when you told me, it came as a shock. I couldn't picture dear old Granny Kath sinning, as you called it time and time again. It shook me, and I'm your generation, not hers! Just didn't fit the woman I'd grown to admire and love like my own granny – may she be resting in peace. You know, somehow if this refugee project develops, I can better see that fitting the mould...'

So it's all wait and see. Right now, he's deep into some investigation online. He muttered he's found something to please my mother. I'll be so pleased. She seems happier now there's a wedding to look forward to and I do so hope that knowing she is the legitimate grandmother of the two boys, with her blood line heritage an' all, an' all, she'll relax.

And I'm relieved he likes my keeping my own journal of progress this way, inserting the summations into Katherine's reports where appropriate as regards the book's finished layout. I trust his opinion: he's usually meticulous in his analysis. Hah! Into the drawer it goes for now. Maybe when I take it out again, when James has sorted through it also, I'll find my path – and a cogent, pithy punchline to draw together all the threads.

Katherine

30

Thursday, 12 October 1933

A letter from Uncle W. He and Aunt Erica are returning to Kendal. He's been offered a lucrative position in Kendal with a legal association in Lancashire. Apparently, some person he met while at Oxford all those years ago has invited him, some long-term project. He writes that as he's now fifty years old it's a good time to cement his prospects, whatever that means. They'll make their base here at the house and he hopes Mrs Smiles will continue to be housekeeper, that I won't run away unless I wish to – 'The house is big enough for us all, Katherine.' Lots to think about. He seems to imply that he and Uncle George aren't getting on since Uncle G married the other woman. Doesn't mention Jacinta and Arthur, or Ralph; nor Rosie. It'll be good to talk when he arrives.

On a brighter note, the big Adelaide store John Martins is to hold a monstrous Christmas pageant in November and it's to be an annual event to raise the public spirit. So declared Sir Edward Hayward, the owner-manager of the department store who instigated this first pageant. It will ride through the city streets and the carts and the fairy book characters will all be made by local people, providing work, jobs and happiness as a bonus. Oh, that is a lovely thought. Uncle W cynically says it will be to herald Christmas spending in his shop but concedes it will be a welcome prospect to brighten up the public spirit after all the miserable years of the Depression.

I also had another note from David. We've corresponded a few times and he writes such newsy epistles I feel I know him quite well. He's been cheered by the news that the MCC has decided there will be no more bodyline bowling in the England–Australia tests. He read in the *Daily Express* that the club will not disclose Jardine's tactics nor Larwood's bowling. There has to be give and take in cricket. Apparently, the teams have been corresponding in a conciliatory manner. I think that will please Uncle W also.

David asks if I would be free the weekend after next and if so he'll book to stay at Mrs Dobson's lodging house. He asks if there's a picture, a film, I'd like to go to or if I'd prefer an evening at the dance hall. I shall look forward to seeing him again. Depending on when Uncle and Aunt arrive here, they may be able to meet. I'd like that.

Wednesday, 13 December

The headmaster called me in today. I knew Mrs P was having some days away; I'd been taking some classes for her. I'd wondered at the legality of this, not being accredited as a teacher, but apparently my record over the last two years has stood me in good stead and I did courses with Mrs P in disadvantaged education. I didn't realise her guidance sessions, as she called them, were in any way official but it seems they were and I've had a boost up the ladder as a result. I was asked if I would care to take the position of an assistant teacher on probation for the first six months of next year, with a review of my qualification suitability mid-year to take effect in readiness for a full qualification after the September start to the following education year. Phew! *Oh, yes!*

I tore home on my cycle to find Uncle W and Aunt E unpacking and settling into the main bedroom they'd used before. Obviously had a smooth trip! Alicia is thirteen and a grown-up little beauty. She's to have the dressing room off her parents' room as her bedroom. I offered mine, even to share, but she's content. It was so very good to see them and nor are there any secrets to hinder chatter between we adults. A jolly evening ensued, with Mrs S relishing the happy company. Uncle W was bemoaning Mrs S's cooking; he describes himself as a body corporate – meaning his increased girth. He obviously ate and rested well on the ship! Aunt E is looking relaxed too, but didn't exactly brim over with jollity.

Uncle W is delighted at the possibility of my gaining a promotion as a qualified teacher. However, later on I caught hold of Aunt E in the hallway. I knew something was bothering her. We sat in the kitchen after Mrs S went up to her little room. My mother's health is what's bothering Aunt E and when she explained, I felt doubly smitten. It seems Jacinta worries her – she wants to leave home to be independent – and Dad is ill with a lung condition caused by wood dusts and other impurities from all his sawing, his woodworking. He has to sit with his head over a steaming kettle for many hours.

Aunt E told me he won't make a long life; however, he could live for years more if he gave up the woodwork, perhaps if they moved to a beach area. I was shocked. He's still a young man, only what – fifty-three. I didn't know of his illness when I sent them one of the new decorated Christmas cards last week, but I did insert what I hoped was a conciliatory note, and signed it with love. Aunt E feels Mum is taking it very badly. Uncle Josh has taken over much of the manufacturing of the business and Ralph is apparently proving adept at the executive side of things, so that's not a worry. But Mum's wearing herself out with nerves and worry and Mrs Blum tries her best but in Aunt E's opinion has lost her edge.

It was too much, having such wonderful news in the morning then this in the afternoon. My nerves tautened and felt the tears bubbling up. Aunt E knows of all the family troubles, so she just moved over to sit next to me and gave me a long hug. I felt guilty because of my own feelings towards Dad, but she encouraged me to remain hopeful. I felt shaken and horribly guilt-ridden. He is my papa after all, my dad. I slept badly; seemed I hardly closed my eyes.

Next day. The headmaster called me and another couple of teachers into his office to discuss who would be teaching what class next term and other organisational chit-chat. For the first time, I really felt part of the system. Mrs P attended, looking thin and pale, but she described what classroom schedules she had anticipated had she stayed on. She was visibly distressed when the headmaster said there had been a discussion about making the school for boys only. Many of the staff demurred. I knew Mrs P's feelings on the matter of girls' education and it seemed others felt the same way. We'll have to wait. I detest the blindness of some bureaucracies!

It was a comprehensive discussion. I was allocated the girls' grade two. I would plan my own schedule, with Mrs P on call should I need her. She actually hoped to attend school at least one day a week until Easter. When I heard the discussion, I sensed this was her preparation for a final goodbye; her illness is terminal. I felt incredibly sad; she's even younger than my dad. He's been given the chance of a few more years why can she not have a similar chance? Surely this radiography can control her disease and enable her to keep doing all her good work? I so needed David to come here and talk and help put my mixed up feelings in perspective.

The boys will be home in a couple of days from their school and Central will be closing on the Tuesday for the Christmas break. The house at Beastbanks will be chock-a-block, busy and noisy again.

I talked with Uncle and Aunt and we decided that if my father died there would be little mourning to be held, other than individually. Uncle was adamant we should not talk as if was likely; after all, he said, people with that terrible tuberculosis are frequently cured with clear mountain or sea air! It wasn't easy; Dad had been my dad for much of my life, stern but fair, until recent years, and I knew much of that was my fault. However, my young cousins had never met Dad so we decided not to mention any of our concerns.

During the festivities, I organised Alicia and the boys to cut out paper chains to stream around the living room for Christmas. I made the flour and water paste – enough to cover all four walls and also criss-cross. It was a noisy, merry Christmas.

I'm not sure how to feel. Just have to wait for word. It's ironic that the work my father loves, working with timbers, could be his undoing. But it had hurt me horribly when he said he didn't want me back there because I'd sinned. I closed my heart to him. I worry for Mum, but if they move away Oma could be losing her son from nearby, and how will she feel? She must be almost eighty now and though I haven't heard that she's unwell it could be too much for her, Dad moving away.

I wonder if his twin, Eloise, is still alive to comfort her mother. She surely could be, they were born in 1880 – sounds a long time ago but Dad's only fifty-three according to my reckoning.

I worry about Mum. So Dad has a chance with clearer air but he won't want to leave Hahndorf; their business and their town is in his blood. However, if Mum sees a chance, she'll work towards it, I know. I'm sure Jacinta will look after her; whatever her trouble with Dad, I'm sure she'll stay loyal. I must write then wait for news.

I'm moving on. It was Stephen's and Nicholas's birthdays on St Stephen's, too. They're now fifteen. Goodness me. They've grown taller this term too and their mum will be surprised when she sees them. Well-mannered, considerate young blokes.

That night, I wrote a long letter to my mum to be posted as soon as the GPO opened after the break.

David came up for New Year and stayed at Mrs Dobson's as usual. Uncle and Aunt seemed to like him and he became more relaxed as we all talked. He and I went out to see the merriment down in the town but it was too late; that merriment was too extreme so we sat in the gardens on a seat, cuddled in his greatcoat. A slight drizzle was falling, the clouds were low, not a star to be seen.

My mood matched the clouds when he stated that the Air Ministry had resolved that Britain 'cannot continue in our present inferiority. Our Air Force must be as strong as any other nation.' I didn't need to ask the question.

He took hold of my chin, looked me in the eye. 'Britain has only 850 aircraft, Katherine. France has 1,650 and the United States and Italy each have 1,000. We're watchful of the threat from Herr Hitler, and our aircraft numbers are to be increased. If so, my darling Katherine, I wish to join as soon as I'm able.'

He walked me home to collect his motorcycle and promised to return the following day. We kissed on the front door step and I clung to him in desperation. After too short a time, he disentangled me from under his now-very-damp greatcoat and I stumbled indoors.

31

1934, Katherine Flack, Assistant Teacher!

I've been very negligent towards you, journal; haven't made any entries for weeks. Lots of reminder notes on pieces of paper, though! My life has assumed a happy routine and my evenings are spent in planning the following day's program for my twenty-two girls. Quite a small class but it seems the Depression is easing, money is flowing and business improving and the children, though still keen on planting potatoes, are obviously well fed at home, and regularly. Some of the girls are keen on planting flowers for their front windowsills and Sally Crescent not far from the school has windowsill after windowsill glowing mostly with geraniums growing in bean and tomato cans, and in Cap'n French Lane the grey-stone walls seem to be sprouting rock flowers from every seam. The boys are branching out into cabbages, it seems. I'm delighted.

I'm even more delighted because this weekend is Easter; in fact, today (29 March) was Maundy Thursday and David is coming up to spend the weekend with us. Because the boys and Alicia are here, he must stay at Mrs Dobson's again. It will be a very special Easter because David, I know, will be asking me to marry him. First he'll speak to Uncle W. Uncle W and Aunt E called me in to talk last night, knowing this was to happen and Uncle W asked if David knew about the baby Avril. I said I'd decided not to tell him, that I believed it would do more harm than good. Uncle thought it was a wrong decision but would accede to my wishes not to mention it. Aunt E agrees with me and she'll say nothing.

I really have thought long and hard about this, journal. There's no medical reason why I can't have another baby. Between you and me, journal (and no one else), we've already indulged in you-know-what a few times since Christmas. David wants to ask me to marry him and I love the man to bits. I will never hurt him.

Good Friday

David came around after lunch and we played cards, a game of 500, we two, Uncle and Aunt. Not for money but for Lucifers, as Uncle called his cigar matches – delightfully old-fashioned. No music on the phonogram – Uncle thought something more subdued for Good Friday more appropriate. David drove off on his motorcycle rather late, will be here mid-morning tomorrow.

Easter Saturday

David was invited into Uncle W's study and after only a few minutes they came out smiling. Not much more to report really – just a lovely warm feeling day. I know we two went for a long walk up and over Fellside and looked over the valley to the Parr castle. The rain had stopped there was a fair amount of blue sky and it was just a *lovely* day!

Easter Sunday, 1 April

Uncle W and Aunt E had spoken last night of attending church this morning, so we all readied for the walk. Alicia wanted to come too but the boys stayed at home. We drank only a quick cup of tea before setting off, David arriving to join us as we were leaving.

'Quite a walk,' said Uncle. 'Missing breakfast means we can take Communion and I'd like that, personally. Don't manage to attend very often. Not at all. Mrs Smiles is preparing a lovely brunch for us when we return. I want to go to St George's, my dears. We went when we were here before, Erica and I.' He smiled at her and she tucked her arm under his elbow.

Certainly was a walk. I was glad to be wearing boots. It took us almost an hour to walk down to Castle Street and there was already carol singing ringing from the doors as we arrived. We shuffled to a long seat at the back. I relished the sit-down even on the wooden pew. The choir was in good voice, the harmonies joyful with a chorus of Hallelujahs! The feeling of well-being and having done the right thing was quite seductive.

After taking Communion, the triumphant old hymns warmed my senses. I felt good. It was Easter after all. I remembered the last time I came here to see the Stillborn Babies' resting place – that struck a sad note. We sang from the hymn books – old, well worn leather covers – and I listened to David's pleasant tenor and turned to him, and he smiled. The man I truly love, and my thoughts meandered to consider coming here for a blessing when we marry.

A tall ecclesiastical figure at the door shook hands with us as we left, none other than Reverend Paulus. He remembered Uncle and Aunt of course and then, horror of horrors, turned to me. 'Welcome, my dear. I hope by now you're fully recovered from your ordeal.'

I stammered something stupid then turned to run as Aunt E firmly guided me out of the door. Thankfully David and Uncle were right behind us.

David took my arm. 'What ordeal?'

Uncle looked him in the eye. 'Oh, she was ill shortly after first coming over – terrible sea sickness, wasn't it, Katherine?'

'But serious enough to have the vicar call?'

Uncle steered us all toward the roadway. 'He was making a courtesy call to new arrivals. Just coincidence. Goodness, doesn't time fly!'

32

Easter Sunday, 1934

Everyone is fast asleep. There's a wind howling outside and beams are and struts are creaking. I'm beyond crying.

After the promised late brunch, I told David. Everything. His face just closed up.

Before we ate, Uncle told me he was done with telling lies. 'I urge you to tell him, Katherine, then just accept the consequences. As you know, that was my advice a number of weeks ago.'

Mrs S had laid on a lovely meal – ham, eggs, fruit, toast – and they all tucked in. David was in a gay mood teasing the boys about football or something, Alicia was protesting that her egg was hard and Uncle and Aunt sat quietly just giving me sideways looks – or that's what I thought. After coffee, David stood and suggested he and I have a walk to look at the garden, so obviously preparing for the moment.

Once through the hedge and out of sight and sound, I stopped him speaking by putting my finger up over his lips. He looked at me, eyebrows raised. Then I blurted it out. I'd had a baby. Stillborn. I'd kept it secret.

That's when his face just closed up. He stood back. 'Katherine! Kath! Am I so gullible, or so wild-tempered that you fear me, that you couldn't tell me this before? We've discussed all aspects of our life together, we've slept together, I love you and respect you. We both have other lives.' He turned and walked down the steps to where his motorcycle was parked.

I stood as he kick-started the bike and roared off. I collapsed to sit on a gatepost. My face was frozen, I couldn't cry.

Then came a hand on my shoulder, Aunt E. 'This had to happen, my dear. It's the right thing to do. Come on, back indoors.'

So here I am, in my room. My life is ended.

Next day, Easter Monday

Uncle W was at breakfast when I went downstairs. Looking up at me, he shrugged then resumed reading his newspaper. That shrug was worth a thousand words to me – soundlessly telling me he was sorry to see me upset but it was my own fault. I poured a cup of tea. David will surely turn up later.

I intend to hang around doing nothing sensible all day long. In case of a note through the door, maybe a telephone call. My sin was not so much my admission as my omission – in keeping it secret. Surely we'd built up a partnership, a real affection? I played with my cup and saucer.

There was an explosion from Uncle W. 'What! Those damned Nazis! What next! You know, Katherine, that Hitler fella's changed the school curriculum so that Jews are marked as a subspecies – that's the children, other pupils, friends in the classroom, all that divisive stuff. These are children, for God's sake!'

'Uncle, I read that they're all being taught a sort of biology in which they measure their heads with a tape measure, check their eye colour and the texture of their hair against charts of Nordic or Aryan types. Then they have to construct their family trees to prove they're not of Jewish ancestry.' I reached for more toast. 'This is all most ominous, Uncle.'

More snorts from his end of the table. 'Hah! One positive move. The antics of that Moseley fella have put him offside with the Tory party and the paper says he's no hope now of winning any parliamentary seats. Hrrmph. Your young protégées at the school, that new family from London…'

'The Ostermanns? Nice young lad. Not too good with English, so that's one of my projects. I can speak my German with him and, though his accent's different, he told me some of what was happening at his school. It was a public one and a new Jewish one was to open up in his neighbourhood but his papa considered it was best not to hang on there and hope for a change in policy, rather to get out to a friendly place. They had to leave their house, though, in the middle of the night with very little money or anything except one special painting his mother treasured. His papa is a doctor and the Nazis had ordered him to go to some institution to conduct medical biology teaching to schoolteachers. Rumours were already circulating about such roles and he decided firmly against it. Officially, he accepted the position but he'd already organised to leave with a former patient who had a fishing boat, the boat owner's family too. The friends are Jewish, every one, but of the Ostermanns only Mrs O is a Jew. The family are all Lutheran, Uncle, like mine in Hahndorf. Because of her Jewishness, all the children were classed as aliens too.'

'Have you heard of more of those refugees arriving here, Katherine?'

'The headmaster has mentioned a movement to bring thousands of children here but there are lots of administrative delays apparently, things like visas and refugee quotas. About eighty per cent of the Jews in Germany have German citizenship but, according to what I've read recently, thousands have already emigrated; many wanted to leave Germany when Hitler became chancellor a year ago, but now things are being tightened up over there. There are also Jews with Polish citizenship that Elena mentioned in her letter, remember? A number of the Polish Jews have been born in Germany and had permanent resident status. It seems that Pieter's mother worked in a newspaper that preached against the establishing of the newer idea of concentration camps.'

'Yes, I read that too. Shocking. The first concentration camps in Germany were established in the weeks after the Nazis came to power, the SA, *Sturmabteilungen*, commonly known as storm troopers, the SS *Schutzstaffel*, protection squadrons—the elite guard of the Nazi party –the police and local civilian authorities organised numerous detention camps to incarcerate real and perceived political opponents of Nazi policy. It was put about that the camps were to be used to "re-educate" the malcontents. Herr Hitler, according to this article, has apparently authorised SS chief Heinrich Himmler to centralise the administration of the concentration camps and formalise them into an efficient system. Rumour has it that SS Lieutenant General Theodor Eicke will have this post but he's also understudy commandant for the extended SS concentration camp at Dachau. The Nazis have already rounded up large number of Jews for such crimes as consorting with German girls or fighting storm troopers and they're interned within compounds bounded by electrified barbed wire.'

He went on, 'Listen to this. "In 1918 Dachau was used by munitions workers, very basic at the least. Now, armed sentries are constantly on patrol and the current commandant, named Wekerle, boasted that "four men recently made a dash to escape and actually made it for a hundred yards before the bullets hit them". So what were they? The camp's to be extended and this reporter writes, "I have been told, quite reliably, that the organisation, structure and practice Eicke's planning for Dachau, imminently, will become the model for the Nazi concentration camp system." Also, I read elsewhere that Eicke fella has as his trainee a certain Rudolf Höss.'

'Uncle, how can you know all this? It's not yet in the papers.'

'You remember the Reverend Paulus? He's an amazing man with some very elevated contacts in this country's government. I spoke with him, albeit briefly, yesterday.'

Yesterday. Oh, my God!

Uncle sat up straight and I think he realised what he'd just said. He folded his paper and laid it on the table. 'Katherine, I said nothing to you yesterday evening for obvious reasons. The Rev was positively excited to know you speak German and asks if you would call on him? He has a proposition for you. Perhaps tomorrow morning?'

I nodded. Can't admit I'm not curious. But that timing will give David chance to contact me. If he's still at Mrs Dobson's. If he wants to.

Tuesday morning, 3 April

'Death warmed up' is how Aunt E greeted me at breakfast the next morning. No note through the door from David; no telephone call. I'd heard nothing from David. During a long sleepless night I'd tormented my brain to forget him. I had cheated on him and yes, I had to take the consequences. It was not a time to sit and mope, as my mother would say. Action of some sort was called for. Maybe this proposition of the Reverend's might serve the purpose. Whatever it might be, I must look ahead. I've closed the door on romance and love.

I cycled down to the church and the Reverend came forward to shake my hand. *'Ich danke Ihnen, dass Sie gekommen sind, Fraülein Flach. Sind Sie bereit für eine Herausforderung?'*

To say I was surprised is putting it mildly. 'Am I ready for a new challenge?' I answered him in my fluent German, no doubt with its Australian accent. Well, it works with Pieter.

He smiled, beckoned me into his living room, and his housekeeper presented us with a pot of German coffee. Yum!

He leaned forward on his elbows. 'I know of your work with the students at the school, Miss Flack.' He grinned, looking almost human! 'Potatoes and vegetable growing on windowsills. Boosting the girls' chances…everything. Including your work for the Ostermann family.' He sat up straight. 'Nazi policy towards the Jews from now onwards is the gradual, social, political and legal exclusion of the Jews from German life. The aim is to make life so difficult for the Jews that they will leave Germany.'

'I have read about it, Reverend. What…?'

'Well, various approaches including violence and intimidation are in play over there by the Nazis. Mainly against the Jewish but not exclusively. Hitler and his unpleasant team are attacking any other nationality not obviously Aryan. Soon after Hitler became chancellor, mobs of locally organised Nazis attacked Jews on the streets. Across Germany many hundreds of Jews were rounded up by local groups and sent to concentration camps. The attacks on Jews soon increased and became more organised. That was last year. Then Hitler realised that the attacks and arrests were random and not controlled by the state. He believes that everything should be controlled by the state, especially the campaign against the Jews. That is the first step, we believe. So over a year ago, 1 April it was, the state organised a boycott of all Jewish shops and offices. The SA stood outside Jewish-owned properties in order to intimidate customers, and shop doors and windows were broken or had the Star of David painted on them. They even made the Hitler Youth do the daubing.'

He went on, 'As part of the boycott, libraries were raided and books written by Jewish authors burned in the streets. In schools, the children were segregated, the curriculum rewritten to reflect Aryan purist gibberish, in my opinion. Latterly, a group of Jewish business men and their wives were forced to scrub the streets in which they lived – to rid the roads of the filth of their shoes, so they were told. With things like toothbrushes and hand scrubbers. Under the whips of a group of the Hitler Youth.'

'With respect, Reverend, I've read of this. I detest what's happening. I know of it from young Pieter, and its personal impact. His Scout group was disbanded and the boys were supposed to enrol in the Hitler Youth. And his father was permitted only to prescribe and treat people of his own blood. Blood? They didn't mean group A or O or whatever. So what was the grand new position thought to be? And Pieter's father is German Lutheran heritage, Aryan through and through. His wife, his children, well… Look at me, Reverend. How can I help you?

'Your knowledge of the language is a distinct advantage. We would like you to go…'

I sat forward on my chair. 'Reverend Paulus, I don't wish to go anywhere! I feel I'm making a contribution to the school. The headmaster says the hospital will be glad of Dr Ostermann and he's hoping…'

'Miss Flack, we know of your additional teaching qualifications and your value to the Central School. A group of us wish to invite you to open a Saturday language school, to teach English to those whose first language is German and also – this may be the most difficult – some of your pupils would be any of the wives and mothers whose own English language education is limited, due to their past circumstances. There would be an emolument. The numbers of refugees are increasing. Some are coming here to England, others going wherever they can flee to, just to leave. America is also a drawcard...'

I couldn't weigh all this up quickly enough. No question, I'd be thrilled to help these people. I feel it would restore to me something of my self-respect – and even Uncle W's. Some expenses would be met too.

'Reverend Paulus, if I could still continue building my relationships with my own school, I would be thrilled to help in any way I can. If the headmaster agrees.'

That grin again. 'Please do not fear on that score. We have already discussed the proposition and agreed. It was mainly your own approval and acceptance that we hoped for. Let me offer you a celebratory sherry please, Miss Flack. The majority would be Jewish refugees but there are some, like the Ostermanns, who are of a mixed culture. We are talking families here, wives, daughters, sons... To the ladies particularly, your knowledge of our social structure is significant. I will be in touch if I may before school returns after the Easter break.'

We shook hands. I collected my cycle and walked it all the way up the hill to home. I needed to think.

33

Saturday, 5 May 1934

Well, it's over a month now and no David, no word of any kind from him. I've been so glad to be busy, to stop me fretting. I always wanted to be a teacher, didn't I, and this couldn't be more different from what I ever imagined. I'm accredited with a diploma for school and now this language school. A touch of home in today's paper too: I've just read that a bust of Adam Lindsay Gordon is placed in Poet's Corner, Westminster Abbey. Wasn't he the man who jumped into Mt Gambier's Blue Lake or something? I'll ask Uncle.

I've just come from my second Saturday school and had a few more members. There are six women, two men and five children. What a mix of levels. To many, I'm Fräulein Flach (with an h) and, to the women at least, I'm Katerin. I'm mentally exhausted. They have Berlin accents and Black Forest dialects and now they'll learn Australian English. It's all a bit unorganised; it's not only a new language for them, it's a culture shock. Well, good luck to them! They're mainly Jewish and lovely people, so embarrassingly grateful for being here. It really does help me with my own self-esteem.

And a welcome surprise! Aunt E asked to come with me on days when she's free. She's a medico and as such can be really valuable. These refugees, the poor souls, have been through some punishing physical as well as mental experiences and I worry about lung conditions among other things – their coughing! Aunt E isn't fluent in Deutsch but seems to understand many of the queries. She prescribes treatments, mainly home remedies they seem to prefer, tells them how to obtain this, that and the other things they need, and I translate from one language to another endlessly, or so it seems, when she has something to suggest and it's working well. She told me on the way home that women want to know what to ask for in the shops; even sanitary wear is new to them. As for our bread!

I really had not foreseen this predicament fully, Aunt E put me right. Being a doctor she intrinsically understands the female condition and is unembarrassed by the most personal questions; it's so good she can be with me. Also, Uncle's pleased that she's happily occupied when her boys are at school. She has made it clear to me that Uncle also admires me for how I've overcome my own personal difficulties.

I'm glad to reach home today, for the early summer weather is abysmal! Rain and more of it. The church hall we use for classes is being painted, windows sealed – victims of age – and lavatories are being installed. Because of the work involved – and all the local workmen are pleased to have the job – the Reverend has suspended classes for the next two weeks. In fact, the next language Saturday will be the 26th.

This break in routine is welcome, journal. I shall have time to plan for the sessions now I have a greater idea of what's wanted from me. If future Saturdays are as mentally rewarding as these seem to be, I'll enjoy the task.

I visited Mrs Peach and she has marvellous advice on specific teaching techniques. She hopes to visit the sessions soon, but her pain is becoming obvious, so I hope, but only hope…and a greater sense of optimism prevails in ordinary conversation. Other than at home. Much of our talk within our own walls tends to be dominated by Germany, the Nazis and the threat of war. Weird contradiction: now I'm encouraged to speak their language when only a few months ago I was being asked not to speak German for fear of local misunderstanding. How things change. Uncle W is horrified at the promotion of Himmler to head the organisation of the concentration camps.

On what is perhaps one of the more optimistic little sides to my life, I'm absorbed in the planning for another tatty pit at school; that project is important too. All nations know potatoes so I'm hoping to welcome some of the refugee children into our planning and thereby strengthen their links with the local students.

I've just read the screeds of stuff I've written, journal – more a book than a journal! I've been home for over an hour and still haven't changed my wet skirt. So much to write to remember. Now here's Mrs S at my door.

'Ave yer seen yer letter, luv? Is it from 'im?'

Later, nearly midnight

Fancy me being too busy taking off my wet boots to look on the little lobby table. There it was, an envelope in David's writing. I tore it open. Mentions the cricket, asks about the family, then asks, so casually, if he can come around and talk this evening about six... Goodness, that's almost the time now! I flew back up to my room and just as I started to brush my hair, Mrs Smiles called upstairs.

I composed myself and walked down, as slowly as I dared. He was standing in the hall, clad in his motorcycle leathers, all shining with the rain. He cleared his throat; nervous? I just stood there, transfixed.

He coughed. 'Hello, Katherine love. I've thought a lot and been busy but so want to talk...'

Not trusting myself to speak in case I bubbled up, I quietly reached for his hand and led him into the sitting room, closely followed by Mrs Smiles and her inevitable tray. I turned around and he held out his arms.

'Oh, Kath. I've missed you so much.'

I couldn't help it. There and then, standing up with his arms tightly around me, I bawled into his shoulder. All the panic, fear, anger and everything else I'd tried to smother within me came bursting out. Then he bent down and kissed me... Oh, how I've missed those kisses.

'Kath, all you've been through and I should have realised how difficult it's been and I was just so miffed because you hadn't told me. Please, Kath, just promise to trust me always from now on. No more secrets. We all have a past and it's our future that I want.'

I put my tearful blotchy face up to his and we kissed. And we kissed.

Minutes passed before he took from his pocket the little package I last saw on Easter Sunday. He held it out to me, opened it and smiled, almost shyly. 'Miss Katherine Beatrice Flack, will you do me the honour of being my wife?'

Well, journal, I'll leave you at that point to speculate further if you wish! With his ring on my finger, a beautiful little diamond circlet, I led him into the kitchen where, almost in a line, Mrs Smiles, Uncle and Aunt were waiting. Then, as he said how I'd consented to be his wife, it was hugs and kisses all round.

Uncle took a bottle of brandy out of the sideboard and proclaimed a toast. 'To the future, for peace and happiness to my dear niece Katherine and David, to all of us and everyone else in this unhappy, angry world!'

Then, as a further seal on my happiness, Uncle grinned and made another toast, as he called it, 'To my absent and well loved sister Esther and her husband, who are, even as we speak, I imagine, settling into their new home in the little beachside town of Victor Harbor, on the other side of the world.'

Mine were uncomplicated and happy tears this time.

Sally

34

26 January 2019

Weeks have gone by since I last looked through the Katherine papers, as James refers to them. His extended sick leave with his busted knee is shortly to come to an end and he'll be off back up to Darwin but on light duties only. I'd hoped he wouldn't have to go up there again. However, he needs to be with his regiment. His physiotherapist is recommending continuation of treatment so that may mean he can stay here a bit longer. He's applied; we'll wait and see. He had a couple of bouts of surgery before Christmas, managed some initial physio and felt reasonably comfortable and able to enjoy all the seasonal festivities. Back into the exercising after New Year and by the time of the wedding he was comfortable standing and walking.

Now that *was* an affair! The parents of the girls had combined, considered, compromised, done all their negotiating. Mine and James's parts seemed almost secondary among all the elaborate decorations and I didn't mind at all. The two girls had chosen individual colour themes. Joanne's was lavender, which Alex matched with his tie; and Ariadne was gold, with Aaron's tie matching his hair beautifully. They each had the one attendant. The ceremony went smoothly; no one cried too openly, so no sniffing in the church.

My mother was fascinated at the history of the Fletchers, Ariadne's family, and at the reception spent quite some time exulting over bloodlines and heritage and wishing Granny Kath could know of the link; she was in her element. The reception was a happy one too, combining the four groups of relatives. It all went smoothly and happily. I just wished my dad, Samuel, could have been with us.

To her credit, my mum was openly demonstrating her pride in

her boys, and I suddenly had a weird feeling Granny Kath was also bestowing an ethereal glow on the proceedings. Alexander and Aaron did look a handsome pair, though, twins so opposite in hair colouring: Alexander's jet-black, smooth and glossy, Aaron's decidedly curly and tending to ginger. Both had shaved for the occasion and that made apparent the marked similarity of their facial features.

'Obviously twins!' whispered Mum, reiterating the obvious to her own satisfaction. I was myself positively glowing in pride, as was James – he hardly stopped grinning!

*

Now it's all over. They honeymooned briefly and are in their new homes, so James and I are on our own. It's a public holiday today but we decided to take it quietly; chances are, he might be posted to a new admin role in Keswick. Not quite to his taste but I'd like him to come home every day like most other office workers. He brought out the Katherine bounty yesterday and has been reading all my notes and her comprehensive, chatty journal entries. She's writing her own story and it's as entertaining as anything I, a published author, had in mind.

I do have a problem as regards turning this into a book. There's too much from the narrator, me, and not enough dialogue. As Katherine's entries are written in extended journal style, that's perhaps logical, but I do like a good balance of dialogue and narration in a book. That's not my only concern, actually. All this information Katherine has about the Nazis and the refugees, it seems insensitive, at the least, to write of it now. In modern terms, after Hitler was defeated, many people from Germany came to live in this country and are all proud Aussies. I've spoken to some and they know about Hitler's campaign against the Jews, but his secrecy, his plotting, was so effective, many citizens at the time knew nothing of the horrors that came to light afterwards. I'm wondering if Katherine had similar hesitations and that's why most of this stuff was hidden in the cushion, she thinking it would be burned.

James is concerned Mum doesn't know of that baby yet. 'Have you told her yet about Avril?'

I have to admit I haven't. Mum herself is doing some digging, in some random way, wanting to link our Fletchers with the new-found Ariadne link, so I'm content not to break into her thinking. Well, that's my excuse.

I'm intrigued to see what may have developed with Granny Kath and David, though. I have some idea, remembering that August chat in her conservatory. I'm still amazed at her secreting all this more personal and at times horrific material in those knobbly cushions. Just when, how long before she died, did she do it? James is less concerned than I; to him, history is history! When I raised my concerns about how Katherine must've felt the need to be circumspect, so hiding the material securely, as she thought, he commented that history is history. Hmm. He was more concerned about how she must have needed some strength to pack this cushion. I notice he's been delving into the depths yet again.

Katherine

35

Still 1934

This seems a long and busy year. David wants to take me to the Tourist Trophy races, known as the TT races, on the Isle of Man. Apparently they're a yearly event, last week of May and first of June – that's for the whole programme. He wants me to go with him and now that we'are officially engaged, even Uncle W has no objection. There's a ferry that takes about three hours over the water from Heysham – that's near Morecambe. School is still busy but I think I can miss a couple of days to go. I'll seek permission on Monday. The 26th might be a problem, I'll need to talk to the Reverend.

Anyway, David stayed overnight at Mrs Dobson's and we'll have all tomorrow together. It's so good to be back with him, I simply hadn't realised how much my secretiveness about Avril might have cost me. No more secrets.

School inspectors want a safety wall repaired and are questioning our tatty pit so the headmaster is busy negotiating and is closing the school while the workers do the wall. That'll be from end of school on the 23rd to the morning assembly on Tuesday 29th. Absolutely propitious! David is booking the ferry for the Thursday morning and we should be there in time for the main racing, he says. He has to be back at school on the Wednesday for an inter-school cricket match. With his bike available, he'll be in good time. His favourite motorbike (as he calls it) is a Norton. They all look alike to me.

This year's senior TT race is the one to watch, apparently. Well, I'm curious, if not fascinated! We stayed at a little boarding house in Douglas that was two shillings and sixpence a night and with a washstand in the room, no bath! David apologised but all of Douglas was packed out with fans and riders. At least the weather wasn't too bad.

That senior TT race was led by a Stanley Woods riding for Husqvarna, but he retired on the mountain section on the last lap after running out of fuel. This handed a junior/senior double win to Jimmie Guthrie riding the works Norton at an average speed of 78.01 mph from another Jimmie, Jimmie Simpson, riding a Norton. David positively whooped in victory!

He explained afterwards that justice had been done, in that Stanley Woods had deserted Norton bikes for the Husqvarna and paid the price for his disloyalty. David had owned a Norton 16H for a couple of years and was looking for one we could both ride on, for trips around the Lakes.

I'm not so keen, journal. He absolutely relishes travelling fast. We didn't have his bike with us of course but managed to walk around the township quite a bit, bought lovely fish and chips, cockles and mussels, and even played the fool on the roundabouts at the fair. A dance was held on the Saturday night and that was wonderful fun.

Being formally engaged, we shared that bedroom and David was concerned I shouldn't become pregnant but, if I did, he promised we would marry as soon as possible. I felt comforted by that. Oh I know, journal, it is the mid-thirties and there are ways to avoid it happening but…well, that sort of strips the mood of any spontaneity, doesn't it? So David says, and I'm quite willing to agree!

Soon, the summer holidays will be on us. I don't know what the church may have in mind for me with the refugees, so David and I can't really plan, although he will have quite a lot of time to himself. He has suggested we motor to his own home town to meet his parents. I'd like to meet them.

Monday, 25 June

School has finished until September. David is still annoyed that I won't drive down on the motorbike to visit his parents. I saw the way those riders on the Isle of Man went round corners. I've seen him speed down the hill from here to Mrs Dobson's! It's all a joke to him, journal, but I'm petrified! When we returned from Heysham off the ferry and we collected his bike to drive home, that was all right till he started showing off. I scraped all the side of my foot and split a shoe. He said I should have just tucked it in. Not pleased, journal!

We've compromised. We'll take the train, wait till the end of the year and possibly spend Christmas there. Nicholas and Stephen will have their parents here so I don't need to care for them.

Anyway, when talking to David on the telephone, he was too delighted at the test result to grumble at me. He'd listened to the second test from Lords, and Hedley Verity took 15/104. Honestly, men and cricket! He's driving up again next weekend. I wish we could sleep together like a married couple but Uncle W and Aunt E are remarkably old-fashioned and there's to be no shenanigans under this roof, says uncle W! We have to be married.

Monday, 6 August

I'm pregnant. I decided to telephone David without delay. He won't be pleased. I waited until I was sure and asked Aunt E to confirm it. Soon the end of the big holidays. The Saturday school continued throughout and the Reverend Paulus wants me to attend a meeting of the Refugee League, as they've called themselves. Some governmental chappies are to come up from London and Liverpool to discuss some new initiatives, as called by the Reverend. I do hope they have some extra help in their planning.

The numbers of refugees are now being allocated to different areas and the problem lies in there being four distinct age groups needing help. It's social, legal, political, as well and lingual! And, journal, I'm so enjoying it. It feels good to help, and these are German people I'm helping. In some strange way, it feels I'm doing this as retribution for my father and my Opa when they were ill-treated by the Australian authorities for being German immigrants in the Great War. When

I mentioned this to Uncle, he raised his eyebrows at me and gave a peculiar smile but I know what I mean, journal!

Proper school has been hectic too. The tatty pit last term was a huge success and a wireless broadcast praised our school for its initiative and the headmaster named me as the primary instigator. Somehow, the reporter found out about my involvement with the refugees too, and the public acclaim has been somewhat embarrassing. The mayor has invited me to speak at a council meeting next Thursday evening. I feel it's all quite unnecessary; my role is a small one, proverbial little fish in a big pond. These initiatives are going on all around the country. Although Uncle W is delighted for me to achieve this measure of prominence (his words), David is not. His school in Lowestoft is a minor public and has quite a different ethos to our central elementary regime, and David seems to be drawing lines between working-class and middle-class. It's an attitude I don't care for.

All this public attention is making the prospect of a wedding rather difficult. I've thought about it and David agrees: we want a civil ceremony. He's not at all religious, but I have my beliefs and would like to receive a blessing from Reverend Paulus on our return from Morecambe – that's the nearest registry. All a bit different from home in Adelaide but quite acceptable in Morecambe. We need witnesses, two at least, but legally there's no requirement for three weeks notice – that was Uncle W's idea. Uncle will drive us into Morecambe and he and Aunt E will witness the ceremony, if that's what it can be called. But it will be legal. That's the main thing.

Mrs Graham came in for sherry with Aunt E last night and told me that Mrs Peach won't be coming back to school next year. I had received a letter from the governors and the headmaster confirming my further appointment for next term and wondered about Mrs P. Mrs Graham is really upset and says her sister's fading; Mr Peach has employed a housekeeper so that Edna can concentrate on her mam's needs. Aunt E has also joined forces with Mrs Graham, and a local nursery is striking peach tree cuttings in honour of Mrs P, two of which will be grown against the school's southern wall in Mrs P's honour. Lovely gesture; prompted my memory of home and I remembered Mum's peach tree up near the workshop on the Hahndorf property: it was regularly loaded with fruit and somehow I doubted the strength of this northern English sunshine, southerly wall or not. Just remembering made me twinge with homesickness. I'm very emotional lately for some reason: tiredness, I think.

I've been helping Edna with some maths; she wants to enter the local hospital for nursing training. She left school too soon when Mrs P became ill and she's been caring for her mother's most intimate needs. I admire the girl and have to say, she seems to have an empathy for the work. She'll need to make up a level in mathematics and with English. I'm glad to help and she's coming on well. Alicia's at our school for another couple of years, then she needs to seek higher tuition to go on further academically, because central is an elementary school. I can help her too, and it really pleases me to know I can give something back!

Also, Aunt E has joined Dr Ostermann on a part-time basis — not Saturdays, though. He's set up a surgery on Stramongate. Uncle has spoken with him a few times and they seem to like each other's company. And, actually, I still don't know what kind of lawyering (Mrs Miles's word) Uncle does! However, he has made a niche for himself somewhere. Nick and Steve are still on holidays until the second week in September and they spend a lot of time on their flashy bicycles riding with friends around the lakes and practising their boating. Nice boys and growing fast.

I've been writing to my mother as often as I felt there was something to say. I've congratulated them on their move and I do hope my dad is breathing easier. He'll miss his timbers, though, although Uncle says he'll no doubt keep up his whittling. If she doesn't reply, perhaps that's because they're too busy settling into the new area. Aunt E says Mum is resigned to my being over here for a while and hopes that their move will cure Dad and also that he'll recover from a depression brought on by Ralph's taking over his business and wanting to make changes. Jacinta doesn't want to stay in Hahndorf now and Arthur too is planning to share a place in the city with another artist friend. Poor Mum – but then Ralph is still there, carrying on the business whether or not he's adapting it to his style. He was always her favourite.

Thursday, 23 August

Cricket's back in the news. Uncle W's delighted that at Headingley Australia have regained the Ashes. Apparently it's due to a record partnership between Don Bradman and Bill Ponsford. Australia cruised to victory by 562 runs to take the series 2–1. 'Hooray,' calls Uncle W. David's eager to discuss the finer points of the game with Uncle. It's a welcome change from the seemingly incessant politics.

However, I wrote too soon. Uncle W is bemoaning the fact this morning over his paper he read that von Hindenburg is dead and Hitler has abolished the title of president and he'll be known for now on as Führer and Reich Chancellor. Seems to be no stopping that man.

David telephoned the Registry Office in Morecambe. Marriage seems all too casual an arrangement. We have an appointment at three in the afternoon on Saturday, 25th. Then I'll be Mrs David Henry Downham. I didn't know his name was Henry, journal!

I also had a very official letter from the league asking if I'd consider travelling to Germany to investigate departure venues for a possible mass exodus of children planned for whenever the war becomes an imminent threat. There were pages of instructions and CONFIDENTIAL was stamped on every page.

A Jewish woman, Lola Hahn Warburg – I think that's the correct spelling – has been organising ways in which Jewish children could escape the victimisation many are speaking of as fact. They're devising ways to be ready for the moment, so Paulus said. They'll need escorts, mentors – official help. When I showed David the letter, he was vehemently opposed to the idea of my undertaking the task, reminding me I'm pregnant; Uncle and Aunt were also against it. It was agreed that our marriage now has priority in our planning and I'll contact the Reverend on Monday after we've married.

Saturday, 25 August

We're married. It was such a simple ceremony, just like a question and answer session really. It felt all anticlimactic. However, all is now legal; we signed the forms, as did my uncle and aunt. Uncle declared it was his first visit to Morecambe without rain. Haha. It's now past eleven at night and I'm sitting at the window looking at a beautiful moon, my journal pages at the ready on the sill, so… I'm turning my wedding band round my finger. It's just a plain gold band, as I wanted. We bought it about an hour before the ceremony. David is snoring in my – our – bed. Goodness, what a noise! I think I'll join him and try to block out his snuffles with my blanket.

Wednesday, 12 September

David rang me to say that airmail rates for post to Australia are now only one shilling and sixpence. He was prompted to ask if I'd yet told my mother about our being married. I do doubt her reaction. She did ask about him. David wants me to send her a photograph. Uncle thinks that would be a soothing gesture. Strange phrase – does he hear more from her than I know? I decided to quiz Aunt E and she admitted they have had a letter or two. They'd been debating whether to respond to her last one with the news of my wedding; now they'll hold off and let me tell her. Thanks for nothing.

I have a photograph that young Edna took of us sitting on his motorbike – only for a short flip down the town, journal. That'll give her something else to grumble about. So I posted it off and when I told Uncle, he was dismayed, telling me she needed comfort and happiness. I didn't know that Oma Kate had died! Uncle said that with my own life becoming busy and complicated, he thought not to tell me as I couldn't do anything other than write in a friendly way to Mum. Well, my letter's not unfriendly. I deliberately held off telling her I'm pregnant…well, because…

I cycled down to the church to see if I could talk to the Rev. and found him with some of his refugee men and older boys. Some he wants me to teach in evening classes so they can tackle proper senior school, which starts the new year in the next few days. Many of the older ones had learned some English in their own Jewish schools before fleeing to this country and were helpful with some of the younger boys. I still feel annoyed at the attention paid to the boys rather than the girls. Mrs Peach knows how I feel and she says things will even out as they spend more time in this country. I do wonder.

I found it really hard biking back up the hill tonight. A muscle spasm in my lower back; too much biking perhaps.

Thursday, 13 September

It's happened again! I've lost the baby, but this time due to an early miscarriage. It's not quite daylight yet but I'm writing this now instead of resting because I feel the little thing deserves recording, although Aunt E said it was too small to determine any sex or anything. I've been awake most of the night but now tucked up to get some sleep, as ordered by Aunt E. I've had a miscarriage; my baby is no more. I want to cry but the tears won't come. David is busy with all the new school year stuff down in Suffolk. We had resolved to work out ways to be together because of the infant. Now that's changed. I shall telephone him tomorrow.

Aunt E insists I rest for a few days, so she'll go to the refuge on Saturday as usual to see how one of the newer translators will cope – a Polish refugee who is a fluent German speaker. She's married to a man who joined the RAF as a youngster a while ago and has been granted a commission, whatever that is. I'll return to Central School on Monday. New academic year, new children.

Saturday, 15 September

David arrived, horribly upset at my losing the infant. Said some cruel things about this house being unlucky, so we should move out! Uncle asked him to accompany him to the refugees; I think he wanted a word. Whatever was said, David met Mrs Pawelski; her husband's of Polish extraction though English, and he was there also. David and he seemed to hit it off, according to Uncle later on. I did notice David seemed more optimistic about things in general, then I realised why: apparently the man is a wing commander equivalent. What's equivalent, I wonder. According to Uncle, their talk was all RAF this and RAF that. Oh, goodness me, it's all war talk but to David it means aircraft.

Uncle is none too pleased at my denigrating war – an opinion I expressed volubly during dinner. His two boys turn seventeen next Boxing Day. If war does become a fact, they'll be right in the catchment age group. I wish I'd kept my mouth shut.

David told me in bed later that the RAF is setting up a Volunteer Reserve, an equivalent of the Territorial Army, and this Pawelski is actually on some organising body. He told David that recruitment posters were being prepared and, depending on the chain of hostilities, the scheme will operate as from the start of 1936. David spoke of nothing else as I tried to fall into sleep; he feels that he can complete teaching the academic year at school and then join, or otherwise. It's all about speed: if it's not motorbikes, it's aeroplanes!

Wednesday, 7 November

Uncle's happy, won quite a bit of money on the Melbourne Cup. Peter Pan romped home again despite torrential rain. Nothing could dampen Uncle's delight. It was apparently quite a festival this year; the state of Victoria has turned 100! And just one thing he mentioned to me seems to indicate moving forward: Jacinta has moved to share a house in Norwood with Arthur.

David drove up and arrived at almost eleven p.m. It was some school governor's birthday holiday tomorrow and, as he doesn't give a lesson this Friday, he's off till Monday! He showed me a draft of the poster designed for RAF recruitment next year. It was headed THESE ARE THE MEN THAT ARE WANTED NOW and one category is wireless operators/air gunners. That's his interest. He seems set on enlisting when he can, if that's the word.

So now the scene is set for the coming year, no baby and more of the same everything else. I feel horribly depressed and, perhaps strangely, I miss my mother. I wish I'd written more cheerfully last time, although I think I was all optimistic about their move. I wish she and I could share a talk over one of her strong coffees.

Sally

36

Monday, 22 July 2019

The year's now well advanced and we're into winter, a very wet one. Every day in July so far, it has rained. My mother has been round this morning, positively chortling in delight because Joanne is pregnant. I agreed, they certainly haven't wasted time! Alexander broke the news to me on the phone last evening. James is back in Darwin after all, so-called light duties that 'bore me rigid, Sal'. We spoke on the phone this morning and he's considering the possibility of an earlier retirement. We talked of plans for travel overseas clashing with staying at home with grandchildren to consider and enjoy. My mother is rapturous about being a great-grandma. What's more, she has been instrumental in the bloodline, in that it's her grandson who'll be the father of another Fletcher descendant. She feels that heredity has provided another link with the Fletcher family.

I've been checking and rechecking my Granny Kath's journal cum novel cum full-length romance. It's disappointing not to have a pithy climax of any kind. I'm almost at the end of all the papers and notes and there's no more detail after 1934. Seems odd. Katherine was so fluent, a natural writer in this, my opinion. Surely there has to be another stash of papers? I know of David's RAF career, his activities, his death; of baby Samuel's arrival in 1941, but only from her verbal account the year before she died. How did she feel when she became pregnant with my dad, when he was born, when David was killed? Why did she stop writing things down in her journal? And what did she do, and where, after the Christmas holidays 1934–35?

Aaron's coming round tomorrow. He's going to read my latest draft of *The Web* to see if it's any good. I think it's a good story but have doubts about it being book-worthy. There is a difference.

37

Tuesday, 23 July 2019

It's quite amazing. Aaron read some of the book and was interested enough to ask to see the old cushion, case, bundles of papers. I decided that the old suitcase could go in the recycling; sentiment apart, it was way past its use-by date. He's also agreed to shred the old cushion for me – it's a hardy, tough fabric, hard to tear. There were a few other papers to pull out for inspection and then he found it.

From the vertical edge of the cushion, where some polymer-type stiffener had been supporting the edging, from the inner lining and at the end of the zipper, he pulled out a plastic ziplock bag. Of all things to find! These bags were only coming into the shops in her last months with us – no ancient wrapping this. So what can it be? Carefully sealed, never intended to be seen, I'd put money on that.

I unzipped it to unpack a collection of smaller squares of fine cartridge paper, covered edge to edge in fine script and glider-clipped together. Inked writing covered one side; on the reverse were diagrams – looked like a city grid arrangement. Some were drawn with a broad nib, others running across were from the fine tip, surely a map or directions of a kind. My mind was racing! Ever since that word *kindertransport* came into the act, I've suspected something more but not that my grandmother would in any way be actively involved. I'd sensed a restlessness in her but that's where it seemed to stay – she was a librarian, for Heaven's sake…

These diagrams, grid references? Too simple? A few arrows denoted direction. From where to where? A starting point seemed to be 'M'. Is this Germany? I know of Mannheim. The written sides carried numbers as if to be read in sequence. On the second, marked with '2',

the main line was criss-crossed; a railway and a dot with a 'K' – Koln?
No; too far south, if M is Mannheim. I found my atlas and traced with
a finger. Koblenz?

Next page, another 'K' – Koln this time perhaps and then, on the
next page A/Hoek. By now I'm tuning in. This could be Amsterdam
and Hook of Holland. On a final page, there's a finger- or thumbprint,
a line drawn through it. A name runs from top to bottom of the paper,
fading yellowy ink this time. Could it be Winston? Or Winton? And,
I think, Paulus. I fossicked out the thumbprint from the tooth powder
tin. It was identical, other than – and this could be important – there
was no line drawn through the whorls of the one in the tin. The print
in the plastic ziplock maps collection does have such a line, indicating a
cut, a scar. Did she have to break something open? That bone manicure
set with lethally pointed ends comes to mind. Just what would that
have been used for? Did she cut herself at a perilous moment? On the
penultimate page of the grid plan the guidance arrows end at 'Lpool
St' – could that be Liverpool Street Station in London? Also bracketed,
(PoL?). Is that querying the Port of London as an alternative?

By now my curiosity was well and truly piqued. Questions flooded
my mind; practicalities seeped into my consciousness. Katherine's
pregnancy failed in 1934 and Dad wasn't conceived till mid-year 1940;
David was away a lot – too much, she had confessed – training and on
manoeuvres; and that left about five empty years, a lot of time to fill. Was
she really the kind of woman to break out into the area of undercover,
spies and espionage? My gran? I remember feeling sometimes when I
visited her that she was holding herself in waiting; there was a kind of
suspense about her, fight or flight. Looking back, those were perhaps the
times she was even less ready to talk. Was she afraid she'd say too much?
And yes, she had that gap – some missing years after all – that will please
my mother but…no… I'll keep shtum until I know more.

Aaron is fascinated by what he sees as a real mystery, as compared
with my mother's constant comments about missing years. 'Mum, I'll
pop round to Granny's tonight and ask to have another look around

the granny flat. This is official immigration stuff, escape from the Nazis. There has to be some other material somewhere.'

Privately, I thought that such official top secret stuff would have been destroyed after the war, not merely stuffed in chair cushions! I doubted his finding anything more but just asked that he let me know of anything worthwhile.

I clicked to a site online, extensive reports relating to the *kindertransport* and the need to extricate Jewish children, mainly, but not all, from the Nazis. Seems the first one under the scheme arrived from a Berlin orphanage into Harwich, England, on 2 December, 1938; that was only three weeks after the dreadful *Kristallnacht*. My knowledge of that event was hazy so I marked it to look up online later.

These first 196 children to arrive on board were from a Jewish orphanage in Berlin and they were met at Harwich by reps of the Refugee Children's Movement (RCM) and eventually placed in foster homes. They were not all Jewish children, nor were all foster parents Jewish, and to me the saddest thing was reading later how they were most unlikely ever to meet their parents again – certainly not the Jewish children.

Initially, most of the children were from Germany and Austria (by then part of the Reich) and in February 1939 trains from Poland were arranged. The plan was that the children mustered in a local area travelled to, then over, the Dutch and Belgian borders then on to England by ship; London and Harwich were the popular English ports but after the German army invaded Czechoslovakia, transports from Prague were hurriedly orchestrated. Planning continued frantically until war was declared on 1 September 1939. Apparently more than 10,000 children under seventeen-years of age were saved from the Nazis in this way. I read then of a Nicholas Hinton mentioned in relation to the *kindertransport* from Czechoslovakia.

'Ahah! Mog! That word on the little maps, not Winton but possibly Hinton.'

Not only England offered refuge; France, Belgium, the Netherlands and Sweden also made room for the youngsters.

Aaron literally burst into my living room next evening. He was waving an envelope, a brown paper envelope. 'Mum, this was under her bedroom floorboards. I think she just forgot it!'

'Floorboards? How on earth! Aaron, this is like one of those hide and seek games.'

'Muuuum! That squeaky one next to her bed she complained about. Not a game – she wanted us to find this. She whetted your appetite throughout, didn't she? First the old suitcase to start you thinking, then the mysterious and fascinating cushion and now this… It's addressed to Samuel, first, then to her mother Esther, second. When did Esther die, Mum? But you can read for Dad. I had a peek, sorry, couldn't resist. Dad will love it… It's written in note form, next thing to shorthand! There's some writing but I left that for you to read.'

For interest SO THAT IT NOT BE FORGOTTEN:

5/3/39 My first time was Harwich/Berlin/Harwich. Final instruction/detail at Berlin hbf luggage drop. Number 2016. Small key, if lost glider clip and hair clip together will unlock found bus instructions. ID for showing to escorts of children from Orphanage. Freight train, basic seating, many on the floor to sleep.

5/3/39 Berlin/Hannover/Amsterdam bus to Hoek Just over 9 hrs. 57 girls, Some non-Jewish. Early teens to max age 17. At Dutch border, children girls given chocolate drink, biscuits. My nerves on edge but these girls permitted to leave so no real risk. German woman Inge help escort. She left at Dutch border. At Harwich number of foster parents. Decent lot, over all. All girls accommodated locally.

9 /7/39 Same route. hbf luggage drop said same orphanage, this time some children from Poland who will meet us at the orphanage, all Jewish. My ID questioned at the orphanage this time, lengthy marshalling of the children. Escort to accompany has come from Poznan – weary, unwashed but all together, The escort was introduced to me as Elena Kalisz – place name and it was my Elena! She older, thinner and with grey hair. I thrilled to see her; no hug allowed. No close contact. Train two carriages, But on travels to Hannover managed to chat. Elena staying in UK. Cannot apply to Australia,

has TB! Not allowed. Asked her to contact us in Kendal. We changed trains at H – all very thirsty and hungry. Hurried scramble to freight carriages again and very brief stop at Dutch border, no chocolate this time. German soldiers at border, quite frightening because talk of we exceeding quota. Amsterdam, military trains coming in. No panic, managed two buses up to the Hoek. Lost contact with Elena. Nearly 10 hours from B. Poznan group exhausted. Ferry gave us all water. I feel physically and emotionally sick. Harwich foster parents too few – some will train to Liverpool Street then to Cornwall.

I was finding it difficult, if not impossible, to accept my so proper grandmother breaking locks, sleeping on freight carriage floors and defying a vicious foreign authority. She so blithely skips over such unpleasantness. Yet here am I as blithely celebrating my children bringing others into this world. I'm totally confused. The horrors of war…surely they'll never return?

Aaron looked at me in consternation. 'Mum, look on the positive side of all this: so many children were able to be saved and my great grandmother played a part. Her devotion to that school and the refugee children turning up there and needing to learn the language before they could learn anything else. Alex and I have wondered about her. That she fought injustice isn't surprising – look how her family treated her after she had that baby Avril. And even her showing kids how to eat better by growing veg… This wartime horror is on another level, sure, but she rose to the challenge, didn't she? She was a brave woman who fought injustice. And key or no key, she opened doors, didn't she? Actually and metaphorically? I think she wanted us to know of her actions, if only the briefest mention. And Dad will be thrilled! Time for a hug, Mum, c'mon…'

So, a comforting big hug and off he went home. I looked at the few remaining unread notes, the last to be pulled out. I needed time to think and tomorrow, very early, I'll skype James…

I picked Gran's photo off the shelf, she smiling sweetly back at me.

'C'mon Mog, into the laundry. Time for bed.'

38

Next morning, 25 July 2019

Barely daylight and I skyped James. By the time he'd absorbed the *kindertransport* activity of his resourceful and indomitable grandmother, he had to switch off and attend – what's it called – reveille? Army life. Said he'd contact me tonight. By then he'll have pondered over Katherine's web of unlikely events.

I pulled out the last loose pages, not anticipating any more surprises. Some were still gummed at the top – good – and secured between two pages was a cutting from a newspaper. No date, but it was headed 'The Children's Transport'. The lord mayor was to award certificates of appreciation to some brave citizen couriers who helped children, Jewish and non-Jewish, from Germany, Poland, Czechoslovakia and Austria to escape from the Nazis from November 1938 until 3 September 1939. Mrs Katherine Beatrice Downham of Kendal was one such person, to be accompanied by her husband Sergeant David Downham of the RAF…

David was with her so it had to have been awarded before 1942. I'm glad he was able to go with her. Which lord mayor? Where? Gran's description implies it's a local newspaper.

Her last actual note before this was written in November 1934. Her descriptions of the escape routes between German and England were dated March and July 1939. My main source of information for the years 1934 to David's death in 1942 remains my brief teatime discussion with her in August 2010. That was when I first realised there might be more to my so respectable grandmother than tortoiseshell combs and lavender cardigans. Yet how I mocked my mother's certainty that Gran had a darker side.

How I wish I could have known of Gran's involvement with the children's transport and told her how much I admire her! Why didn't she tell me, all of us, so we could have told her how we admired her? Surely not modesty? Was it restrained because of an Official Secrets Act? What was termed classified information? I can't think so when it was broadcast in a newspaper that she was given a certificate of appreciation, as I assumed was given to all the other participants. That was some time after 1939 and definitely before David was killed on active service.

I was still debating this when I unfolded the telegram. It was stained pink-tinted paper and its ink was faded but it had no loss of impact for all that.

FRIDAY AUGUST 17/45
REGRET MUM ESTHER KNOCKED OVER BY HEAVY CART ON HIGH STREET DIED THIS MORNING IN ADELAIDE HOSPITAL. TELL UNCLE W. RALPH

Oh, poor Katherine on receiving this. She wanted to make up some time with her mother. Esther died before her daughter Jacinta who drowned in the ice of 1947. Is that why Jacinta spiralled out of control? I hope Katherine had started writing to her mother more frequently as she promised after she married and so told Esther about her involvement with the children's transport. If it was in newspapers before David died, there is a chance…

Oh, how did she feel? Then a notice dated 13 May 1945. Going backwards… I've forsaken James's recommendation of adhering to a chronological order – not always practical.

Katherine

39

Sunday, 13 May 1945

Journal, this war is all but over. Years have passed. The wireless talks of huge celebrations in Whitehall. There was cheering as Winston Churchill drove by on his way to lunch at the palace. Then as Big Ben chimed out three o'clock, the prime minister announced over the speakers that although Japan still had to be subdued the war in Europe would end at midnight. The announcer said it was the signal for the release of years of pent-up feelings. Then he laughed as he said the crowd had gone mad, kissing and hugging and dancing and forming hokey-cokey parades! We listened to it all in Beastbanks and Uncle opened his whisky again for a toast.

I've spoken to Uncle and Aunt E at length over the last few days. I want Samuel to grow up in Australia. Shipping is assuming a normal pattern again and I want to go as soon as possible. I have about fifteen years to make up with my mother. I want to see Jacinta and the children Aunt E speaks of. Jacinta and her children could live with me, in a suburb of Adelaide; they're building new houses out there. Uncle understands and he's planning to sell up the Kendal house; he feels it's served us well, but he still has his house in Adelaide, and Steve and Nick want to emigrate, as they call it, despite being born there.

Mum still lives in Victor Harbor but Dad's buried in Hahndorf as he wished. He had those extra years in Victor, we know, and Uncle knew from Mum how he enjoyed his garden there, but he wanted to be buried near Oma and Opa. Hahndorf was his home town, after all.

Aunt E suffers from arthritis in the cold winters in Kendal and wants the warmer climes – Uncle's phrase. Their two boys acquitted themselves well in the war, came through safely, thank God. They met some Aussies in the RAF and 'responded to our egalitarian ways' laughs Uncle, smiling. Alicia is now working as an intern in a hospital in Lancaster, following in her mother's shoes, and has indicated she will return to Adelaide when her parents do.

I think it's time now to end my diary notes. I've written about my time away from Australia as much as I want to. I can't go back to Hahndorf, other than to visit the graves. I don't feel I belong there with Ralph at the helm, and he married Kris's sister after all. I do not want to reconnect with that part of my past. Except Jacinta. I know so little of her and I presume she's still over there, though she's a 'free spirit and longing to travel' – Mum's words last time she wrote.

Jacinta has not written to me since that angry letter when she blamed me for Dad's anger. I think I'll try to reconnect with Rosie – she and I shared quite a few endeavours over here – but first I must buy a home for me and Samuel. I shall then hope to enjoy a quieter, less eventful life, perhaps as my mother always hoped. I've written to her, telling her of my plans, and something of my teaching and my involvement with the refugee school. Not the other business – can't write about that. I feel if she knows about the schools it might be some retribution for the way in which my past behaviour caused her distress. It's so long since I saw her, when we meet I want to be able to speak frankly and openly and make up a little for my past neglect of her.

I shall keep my diary notes, if not the later ones. One day they may be interesting to someone in the family. Maybe.

For now, journal, *auf wiedersehen!*

Sally

40

Tuesday, 30 July 2019

I'm waiting at the Adelaide airport carousel for James. He's glad I've finished the book. So am I, but was it a successful strategy to allow her to use her own words? I feel she was owed the memoir, because hiding behind her age, perceived ordinariness – lavender cardigans, silver-gold hair with its tortoiseshell comb and above all that sweet smile with just a suggestion of mischief at the corners – lived a woman who was anything but ordinary. How I wish I'd known her story to talk with her about it. It's truly amazing, considering…

I'm still assessing the mechanics of its telling. Fellow writers understand: chapter order; inserted paras or not for each writer; too many exclamation marks…the list goes on and on. Most of all, is it an interesting tale for the reader? Does Katherine appeal? Are my intermittent comparisons of my own life enough to stress the differences? So much tidying up to yet be done to make it into a worthwhile book, meeting the recognised criteria. However, I have a meticulous editor in my James. He can be pedantic but it's a blessing in my writing.

Here he comes. Big hug, good to see him, and he's home on two weeks leave, final physio check-up for his busted knee. We'll make good use of the time. The family awaits us for a start and because we missed James's birthday on the 7th, we'll enjoy a family dinner this evening. Great.

'Sally, lovely to be home. So, finished the magnum opus? And, before we catch up, how's your mum feeling about it now she knows of the little Avril?'

'Oh, no problems at all, James. And you know what is so delightful?

You know how Mum felt deficient and I pulled up her family history to feel better? Well, now she has the ultimate accolade, so she feels.'

'Howzat, Sal?'

'Ariadne's Fletcher line seems certain to be the one from which sprang the matriarch Beatrice, grandmother of Katherine, no less. Now that Mum's great-grandson infant when born will share that bloodline, Mum feels equal, if not more so, than any of us in the line of heritage. She talks of things going full circle. Her delight is almost comical, James, but so refreshing!'

He laughs – usual lovely bellow as his bag zips by on the carousel. It's infectious; still smiling, we walk over to the lifts and up to the car.

'You know, Sally mine, it's so strange the way things work out in life. I doubt your gran ever told your father about her exploits in Europe, about how she was able to help rescue so many children. If he knew, in saying you were carrying on the line of strong women, wouldn't he have marvelled at his mother's initiative – her bravery and commitment in helping to rescue the children?' He grinned. 'Then told you all about it in detail.'

We're soon driving home. He's sitting quietly, just thinking. I know he's weary.

He pats my knee. 'I do feel it's been a journey for you, Sal. Sometimes a wayward search for truth but you persevered. You had the instinct for a story and dug until you found it, hidden though it was within that most unlikely character. Then you pursued the facts, as many as could be revealed. But what a magnificent woman she was. Her loyalty to whatever secret service swore her to secrecy was outstanding, if frustrating for you. And her actions were more deception than deceit…'

He yawns. 'There is a difference, you know. Her reticence, I feel, came from a desire to do well whatever she was charged with and to avoid giving hurt, at any level. She knew what hurt was, your Katherine.' Yawning again! 'You took on a challenge, love, not easy, but to use your mother's analogy, you travelled the full circle. I'm really looking forward to reading the parts of Katherine's story I had to miss when I was away. Now, remind me: has its title been decided? I remember you took a phrase from *Marmion*…'

'*Katherine's Web.*'

'Spot on! "Oh, what a tangled web we weave…"'

Acknowledgements

Works consulted

Brown, R. Douglas, *East Anglia* (War Series), Terence Dalton, Lavenham, Suffolk

Ross, John (editor), *Chronicle of the 20th Century*, Chronicle Communication and Penguin Books Australia

Exhibition guide: The Holocaust Exhibition, Adelaide University Union Gallery, 22 April to 2 May 1982

Dedicated online sources consulted

JC Williamson (Firm) – Trove – National Library of Australia: https://trove.nla.gov.au/people/568370 James Cassius Williamson/ Australian Dictionary of Biography-ANUadb.anu.edu.au/biography/ williamson-james-cassius-4859

Kendal National School, later Central School, grid ref: SD513925, Beast Banks, Kendal, Cumbria, UK: https://www.visitcumbria.com/ sl/kendal-nationalschool

Kindertransport Association/History: www.kindertransport.org/history. htm

Kindertransport/European History/Britannica.com: https://www. britannica.com/topic/Kindertransport

Thanks

Special thanks are owed to my publishers and editors Stephen and Brenda Matthews of Ginninderra Press for their unfailing professional guidance; to my friends and colleagues of the Tea Tree Gully Library Writers Group and NEW Inc. for their collective and continuous encouragement; to the Tea Tree Gully Library for their continuing support of local writers; to my family for their tolerance; and, last but not least, to Phred for his meticulous proofreading, his patience and his (hopefully deserved) confidence in me.